Stephen An

'Heartbreaking and haunting but filled with a silent strength as well, this collection is brimming with all kinds of complex emotions and yet is compelling enough to read in a single sitting. Absolutely loved it.'

**Awais Khan, author of *In the Company of Strangers*
and *No Honour***

'From the heart-wrenching dedication onwards this incredible book lures you in. I was moved, shocked, heartened and totally absorbed by these uniquely compelling stories. Stephen is an incredible writer and I hope he writes a lot more.'

**Paul A. Mendelson, BAFTA-nominated
screenwriter and author**

'It's a thoughtful, reflective and beautifully written collection about the extraordinariness of ordinary people's lives. It feels like all of the human experience is here, the sad moments, the happy times, the dark side, and the bits in between - the stuff that binds us all together and makes us understand what it means to love and to live. It's a fantastic book for dipping in and out of - I took it travelling with me - and there's some memorable characters that will stay with you long after you've finished reading. It's one of those short story collections where all the stories seem to combine to make a whole. Recommended!'

Ali Harper, author of *The Disappeared* and *The Runaway*

Borrowed Time

Stephen Anthony Brotherton

First published in Great Britain in 2025 by
The Book Guild Ltd
Unit E2 Airfield Business Park,
Harrison Road, Market Harborough,
Leicestershire. LE16 7UL
Tel: 0116 2792299
www.bookguild.co.uk
Email: info@bookguild.co.uk

The manufacturer's authorised representative in the EU
for product safety is Authorised Rep Compliance Ltd,
71 Lower Baggot Street, Dublin D02 P593 Ireland (www.arccompliance.com)

This work is entirely fictitious and bears no resemblance to any persons living or dead.

Typeset in 12pt Minion Pro

Printed and bound by CPI Group (UK) Ltd, Croydon, CR0 4YY

ISBN 9781835743317

British Library Cataloguing in Publication Data.
A catalogue record for this book is available from the British Library.

Thank you to Paul Francis for his coaching and mentoring skills. Without his help, this book would never have come to life.

Thank you to Awais Khan for his supreme editing skills.

This novel is for River, a schnoodle who came to me through the draw of a fate card and now exists as a permanent feature at my side. She's had to listen to the creation of every word of this story over and over. I think that means she deserves some recognition.

The Cast

Gods:	Humans:	Pets:
OCTAVIUS (EMPEROR)	RICO	WANITA (CAMEL)
HELENA (EMPRESS)	MARY	GERTIE (OWL)
LIVIA (PRINCESS)	FATS	GROWLER (URCHIN)
SEBASTIAN (LIVIA'S MANSERVANT)		PENELOPE (HARPY)
ATHOS (GOD OF WAR/MEMBER OF THE ECCLESIA)	BERNARD (MONK/ MEMBER OF THE ECCLESIA)	GOSHAWKS
TIMUS (GOD OF STRATEGY/ MEMBER OF THE ECCLESIA)	JETHRO (SMOKE HUMAN)	ORB (LIVIA'S)
DARIUS (GOD OF MESSAGES/ MEMBER OF THE ECCLESIA)	MICHAEL (SMOKE HUMAN)	TALKING CAT
PHILLIPPA (GOD OF FATES/ MEMBER OF THE ECCLESIA)	ALFIE (SMOKE HUMAN)	

The Cast
(continued)

Gods:	Humans:	Pets:
CICERO (OCTAVIUS'S PROFESSOR)	THOMAS (SMOKE HUMAN)	
PALOMA	PSYCHO JEAN	
SINI	RICKY NO TOES	
CAPTAIN (JINGA)	SOLDIER (CRYSTAL ONE)	
HECTOR (JINGA LIEUTENANT)	CHUG BOATMAN (CRYSTAL TWO)	
AUGUSTUS (JINGA WARRIOR ONE)	FIREMAN (CRYSTAL THREE)	
ANTHONY (JINGA WARRIOR TWO)		
WRATH (DEVIL)	GRACE (CAFÉ OWNER)	
BEELZEBUB (LORD OF THE FLIES)	BARMAN	
WOMAN ON THE BEACH (LIMBO KEEPER)	GEMMA (JEAN'S GRANDDAUGHTER)	

Prologue

A game of cards. Nothing more.

That's what Livia thinks when they leave the atrium, but when she thinks about it later, she should have known it wasn't an ordinary day. For a start, Father is happy – he's been whistling something tuneless all morning. He even attempted to tickle her at one point, which didn't really work because he did it awkwardly, barely touching, like acting out a mime. Practical stuff. That's what Father is good at. Chasing moons, surfing clouds, not tickling.

Mother gives him a puzzled expression. 'You're in a good mood.'

He laughs. 'I want to savour the day,' he says, ruffling Livia's hair and waving them into their individual glass transport pods.

Savour the day, thinks Livia as she waits to be shot to the surface of the planet below. *What does that mean?*

Seconds later, the doors of the pods swish open and they step out into a glade, a crowd cheering as they walk across the grass towards a makeshift stage. Livia sneaks a sideways look at Mother, tries to copy her graceful, confident steps, like a panther strutting across a prairie. Father stops them halfway, tells Livia to wait, but he frowns when Mother takes her hand. 'She's too old for that,' he says. Mother squeezes her hand tighter. He shrugs and strides towards a card table set up at the edge of the forest.

Dewy grass dampens Livia's bare ankles as she walks the rest of the way lost in her thoughts. Perhaps ten is too old to be holding Mother's hand. Maybe the emperor's daughter should behave differently, be more grown-up, even when she's not.

They take their seats, Livia sitting up straight and smoothing her baby-blue cotton dress down her legs. She nods regally in the direction of the crowd, and a human boy, about the same age, bows in her direction. Mother gives her a squeeze and strokes her hair. 'You okay, darling? Not too hot?' Livia looks up and shakes her head. Two suns glow high in the sky, but she's protected from the heat by the canopy covering their thrones. Mother touches Livia's forehead, but she shakes the hand away, conscious that Father might be watching.

He reaches the table and Livia wonders if he's still savouring the day. He looks happy, smiling as Uncle Wrath rises from one of the two seats and they shake hands. The crowd hushes when they sit, and the game starts, a soft warble of birdsong leaking in from the surrounding forest. One of Mother's maids kneels, touches Livia's arm and passes her an ice cream. She takes it without saying a word and licks it lightly – mint choc chip, her favourite. She hears Mother start to hum songs she's heard the minstrels play in court with their sitars. Gods and humans together, basking in a fun day out, watching their emperor play cards. All is safe and well.

And then a gasp from the crowd makes Livia stand. Her cone falls to the floor, sploshing ice cream across the oak boards of the stage. Father jumps to his feet and gives Mother a panicked look. Uncle Wrath laughs, scratches the horn in the middle of his forehead and then bangs on the ground three times with his staff. Father grabs Uncle Wrath's hand, says something to him, looking at him with desperate eyes, but Uncle Wrath pushes him away and bangs his staff again.

The ground starts to vibrate.

Livia looks at Mother, who leans down and kisses the bridge of her nose. 'I love you,' she whispers. 'Your father will look after you.' And then she walks towards the table, all the crowd looking at her. Father mouths 'sorry' in her direction, and Uncle Wrath laughs once more.

'Mother,' shouts Livia. 'Mother.' But she keeps on walking, not looking back, like she's in a trance. Someone – one of the Jinga, Father's bodyguards

– puts a hand on Livia's shoulder to stop her from moving. 'Let go of me,' says Livia, giving the man a hard stare. 'How dare you touch a princess.' But the man just smiles and tightens his grip.

The ground vibrates again and this time a pencil-line break wriggles across the grass, forcing itself wider and wider. Another gasp from the crowd as something pokes through. Ram horns followed by a head and then a purple, swollen face with bulging eyes, swivelling to take in the landscape, and a serpent's tongue flicking the air, tasting the freshness of daylight, frothy spit oozing and bubbling before falling to Earth.

Livia puts her hand to her mouth. It can't be. Father told her it didn't exist, but here it is. An image from her nightmares, pulling itself out of the ground, its lizard tail slithering onto the grass.

Mother walks towards it.

Why isn't she stopping? Livia looks at Father. *Why isn't he doing something? Just standing there shaking his head. How's that going to help?* 'Mother. Mother.'

Beelzebub. That's what Father had called it when she'd told him about her dreams. Made up to frighten children. Not real. Well, here he is, a fairy tale looking at Mother like she's a juicy crumpet with butter oozing on top. It throws its transparent bat wings skywards, sniffs the air with its antenna and howls to the clouds. And then it starts to thud towards

Mother, forcefully placing each step, Frankenstein's monster style, dragging its hunched, withered body across the grass. Mother calls something to Father that Livia can't hear, but then she carries on walking towards the demon. That's what he is. A demon. Lord of the Flies. That's what the legends say. A myth, but he's heading for Mother, the break in the ground following him like a tracer.

Livia hears Uncle Wrath shout, 'Get on with it.' She looks over. Father has sunk into his seat, head in his hands. She turns to Mother again. 'Mother. Mother.'

At last, Mother meets her eyes, a gentle smile spread across her lips. She goes to say something, but Beelzebub quickens his pace, connects his brain and legs, reaches Mother, coughs and smothers her in phlegm. Mother screams, which makes Livia scream.

Wrath thuds his staff again and the crack landslides into a hole. 'Go,' he shouts.

Beelzebub wraps his wings around Mother, and they fall through the earth.

Livia stares at the woods and then back at Father.

He's just sitting there, watching Uncle Wrath hold his celebratory hands skywards.

I

Fats knows his time has come the minute Ricky No Toes hurls him from the bimmer's boot and he lands with a thud on the gravel car park.

He looks up at the derelict gala baths towering above him. The Execution Centre. A place of no return. He's been here before, but on the other side of the fence. Now, he's fucked. The only question is how quick. His preference would be a shot to the head, but screwing Jean's eighteen-year-old granddaughter probably means being hunted by Rottweilers around the empty pool until they catch him and rip his flesh into party streamers. A spectator sport, with Jean and her posse sipping cappuccinos as they watch from the gallery.

'You little shite,' snarls Ricky, kicking Fats in the ribs. 'I'm going to enjoy your screams.'

A Merc screeches to a stop next to them, its tyres spinning on the gravel.

Ricky steps back and grins. 'Showtime.'

The driver's door opens; red stilettoes and long legs in burgundy leather trousers drop onto the car park. Fats closes his puffy eyes and thinks about saying a prayer. He hears the doors on the Merc slam shut, then crunching gravel as footsteps head towards him. Breath touches his face, and the cloying smell of white musk perfume hits his nostrils. 'Look at me, Fats.'

He opens his eyes.

She's kneeling at his side, heavily mascaraed lashes, pink lipstick, spiky blonde hair, a sea of gorillas at her back staring down at him. 'You're dead. You know that? She wasn't even born when I first screwed you.'

'I'm sorry. I—'

She grabs his groin and crunches his balls in her fist. 'This is your fucking problem.'

Fats screams.

'Get the cutters. We'll take these as a starter for the dogs.'

One of the gorillas walks over to the Merc and opens the boot.

II

Mary bangs her head on the pillow, willing sleep to consume her.

She's spent the last two hours listening to Rico snore at her side, wondering if he's dreaming. He never worries, but she feels a dread dropping like a blackout curtain. Nothing specific, not yet, but a rolling gripe in her stomach and a whisper in her head tells her an east wind is rising and heading their way. She knows from childhood Bible studies that an east wind means God's wrath crashing down on them. Divine punishment. Her dad's pet subject. 'He sees everything. He'll catch you in the end.' Insomnia ruled Dad's life, and he'd wander the house at night, looking for jobs to keep him occupied. She'd once come down for a glass of water and found him cleaning all of their shoes, lining them up on the kitchen carpet like he'd started a new industry. 'What are you doing, Dad?'

'Cleanliness is next to godliness, Mary.'

She shakes her head, turns her back to Rico and

closes her eyes. A weariness spreads through her body. At last, here it comes – much needed rest.

She tumbles in water, a dragging tide pulling her against the current, falling, falling, air bubbles streaming past on their journey to the surface. Something's not right. She's breathing, but she should be drowning. Down, down, down. And then water morphs to clouds, and she's still falling, the ground zooming closer, closer. She braces for impact but knows she's doomed. Here it comes. Three, two, one. The earth opens up, swallows her into a hole. Rock formations hurtle by. More ground below. Trees. Eucalyptus. Something slows her descent. She floats in the breeze, heads for a clearing, a sun-dappled glade in the middle of a forest, and a cushioned landing on thick, luscious grass.

She turns towards a noise at the edge of the trees.

Breaking twigs.

An image floats towards her.

A Goliath, white hair and beard.

He sits on the grass and beckons her with shovel hands. 'We need to talk.'

III

Rico's eight-mile daily run takes him across farmers' fields, up and down meandering hillsides and along dirt tracks, pulling at his muscles and sucking his lungs dry. It's circuitous, naturally bringing him home, and gives him a chance to reset his mind, remind him of where he is in this new world. He likes the changing seasons – shedding maple trees in autumn, fiery dogwood in winter, everything bursting and budding in spring, sweet-smelling eucalyptus in summer. It's all there along his route. And he has Springsteen for company. A new discovery.

He presses the buds tighter. The soundtrack reaches 'Dancing in the Dark', telling him he has a mile to go. The thought of Mary quickens his pace. She's been different of late, more distant. He needs to up his game, get them back on track, perhaps a break away. They've dared not leave the farm, and then there's the dogs and Wanita. *It'll be fine*, he thinks. All couples go through these phases. They need a change of routine, something new. Adrenalin surges through his body. It's baking day today and she'll smell of warm bread, with single-portion apple crumbles lined up in ramekins on the work surface, mostly buttery biscuit, hardly any fruit, exactly as he likes them. 'Crumble crumble', she calls them.

Not that she'll be in the kitchen by the time he's finished running. She'll be waiting in bed, naked, soft skin lying on a warm, crumpled sheet. That never changes. She likes him sweaty, straight out of his T-shirt and shorts, his body hard from exercise. He quickens his pace, makes his legs go faster, digs deep as he starts to surge up the final hill, followed by a downward sprint to their farm. He ignores the pain in his chest as his lungs gasp for more oxygen. Mary's knees, thighs, her flat stomach with a belly bar glinting from her navel. He almost trips on a stray branch from the brambles growing alongside the dirt track. 'Calm down,' he tells himself. 'Better to get there in one piece.'

Suddenly, it's in front of him. The single-storey, wooden farmhouse they've called home for the last five years. He touches the ring on his left hand. A white gold band covered in bridge and spot diamonds. A gift from the princess. His princess. He instinctively looks across at the outbuilding. Wanita, their grunting camel, browses on the eucalyptus trees they've planted for her, and dogs bark from inside individual kennels, created to provide sanctuary for abandoned pets. Everything is right with his world.

And then it starts to rain, and his finger beneath the ring begins to itch.

IV

Livia slumps on a platinum throne in a top-of-the-world glass atrium and catches her reflection in one of the arms.

Her temporary titles drop into her head: *Arbiter of Fate. Supreme Commander. Soul Sorter.*

Two meteoroids blaze across an ink-blue sky in front of her. She hopes it's a couple of the souls she's pardoned, given the chance of another existence – a mercy rarely granted when humans are brought to account for their lives, her father, Octavius, frowning on such leniency. She looks through glass walls at Octavius's favourite planet, the one occupied by humans who, for millennia, have been bred for entertainment, their lives played out on nightly soap operas – gods manipulating fates for fun.

Games, not tickling – everything a competition and on the clock. Her father's area of expertise. And that's what he'd said to her through the plasma pool. 'Let's play again, Livia.' As though she had a choice. Her mother used to say he couldn't smile, had a face like a cracked Toby jug or a church gargoyle. She'd make Livia snigger by puffing her cheeks out behind his back. He could be loving, but games changed him – an ever-present trial to test her ability; to sharpen her skills. Sucked of fun by his seriousness. 'Come out, come out, wherever you are.' Hide-and-seek. His chant getting more and more urgent as he prowled the palace looking for her. 'Come out, come out, wherever you are.' Her waiting in a cupboard or under a sofa, expecting chastisement if she didn't beat her best time to stay hidden. And now, a new game. Chasing humans. Chasing her champion. She'd beat him last time, and he wanted revenge. 'Let's play again. You know you want to.'

One of the teller sisters, Paloma, cackles and brings Livia's focus back to the far end of the atrium. The other sister, Sini, stretches her wrinkled fingers and coaxes raw thread through a whorl-weighted distaff. Paloma, tall and thin as a pipe cleaner, strides up and down the glass floor, threading yarn along a gold-framed loom to create warp and weft scenes of human existence. Here's a man being chased around an empty swimming pool by two dogs; next to this a stone tower with a pinprick of yellow light trickling through an attic window. And in another scene, a naked human male with a washboard stomach and black hair pulled tight in a ponytail. He's lying on a single bed set up on an attic floor.

Paloma snips a thread, steps back and cackles again.

A door slams and Sebastian, Livia's eight-foot-tall, albino manservant marches towards the throne, anxiety carved into his face. He comes to a halt at the side of his princess and bows. 'Your Majesty. We must—'

She raises a finger and glares at him.

'I was only—'

'Be quiet while I watch my fates work.'

He scowls, bites his lip and stares up at the glass ceiling. He looks again at the princess. She's still glaring at him. 'Your thoughts are intrusive,' she snaps. 'What's the matter? Say it, quickly.'

'Your champion,' he says, crouching down and drawing his hand over the plasma pool at his feet, bringing a rippling image of a man in T-shirt and shorts to the surface. 'He's at risk.'

'Octavius has found him?'

'Not yet, but something blocks the woman's image. It can only be the emperor.'

She walks over to the loom and traces her finger round the woven man lying on the attic floor. 'At least we have a plan. Will this gangster be up to the job?'

'I believe so.'

'A shame he must be sacrificed, but he's disposable. Let us get started.'

Sini and Paloma bow in unison and resume their weaving.

V

Fats wants to open his eyes, but the thought of what might be out there tells him to bide his time. His last memory is of Bloater, Jean's stud dog, lunging for his throat, white eyes rolled back in its head, drooling jowls, like a scene from a horror film, tearing clumps from his flesh as it chased him round the swimming pool. He'd wanted to stand still, but instinct made him run, giving Jean and her beefy boys their showtime, the bastards laughing and clapping as he clawed at the concrete walls. At least she'd not snipped his balls. 'I want you fit to run,' she'd said, 'but I'll take them later, have them framed.' That fitted her MO. Gossip had her in possession of three dicks in her loft, trophies gathered from ex-lovers who'd crossed her.

He touches his groin, feels his tackle and lets out a sigh of relief. He suddenly becomes aware of his nakedness and remembers Jean stripping him. 'It'll give the dogs better access,' she'd said as Ricky No Toes kicked him into the empty pool. The dogs had looked bemused, like it was a mistake, that Fats should be ringside, but they'd snapped into pursuit when Jean shouted the command.

Dead.

He feels the softness of a mattress beneath him, senses he's in some sort of room. He never expected this, but then he'd never thought about it much. Heaven or hell. By rights, given his lifestyle, he should be feeling flames right now. Maybe that was for the best. Fucking God botherers. He once saved his piss in a bucket just to chuck it out the window over a bunch of Jehovahs on a Sunday morning. Maybe they're here. That would make things interesting.

'Open your eyes, Marty.'

A man's voice, calling him Marty. No one uses his real name, except his mum. She might be waiting for him. Maybe that's what happens… you go back to your mum. The thought makes him tremble. All those years locked in a coal shed, shitting himself in the dark, tiptoeing round her weirdness, biting his lip while she strapped him with a dog lead. Another reason not to open his eyes.

He flinches as a hand touches his arm.

'Time to wake up, buddy.'

Fats does as he's told.

A face smiles down at him. Unshaven, piercing pink eyes, completely white hair and skin sucked of blood. 'Welcome to the afterlife,' the face says, putting his arm round Fats' shoulder, pulling him into a sitting position and turning him off the bed.

'The afterlife…?'

'Sure. What did you expect? I'm Sebastian. You'll be fine in a few minutes. It takes a while to come to. Let's get you sorted. You need to look your best for your audience.'

'My…?'

'With the princess. You've been chosen, pal. One in a million.'

'I don't…'

'You'll see,' says Sebastian, laying out a pile of clothes on the mattress. 'Time to get dressed.'

Fats pulls the band tighter round his ponytail and looks round the room. White floor, walls and ceiling beat back at him. The bed is the only item of furniture. 'Where am I?'

'We've done that one. Get dressed.'

A change in tone. An order not a request. The albino looks pissed, and Fats doesn't know why. He tries to pinpoint something he might have said. He picks up the boxer shorts on top of the pile and pulls them up his legs. The rest of the clothes are fit-boy, which suits Fats, his nickname ironic because of the six-pack cultivated over years in the gym. Jogging bottoms, purple running shirt, a pair of light-blue trainers. He dresses quickly, conscious of the albino towering over him. *You're the stranger here. Be careful.* He ties the laces of the trainers and stands.

'We're late,' says Sebastian, striding towards a door at the far end of the room.

Fats takes a last look round his afterlife arrival point before following.

VI

Mary kneels in front of a log fire and stares into the yellow and blue flames as they're gently tugged up the chimney stack. Rain hammers against the windows, and she sucks in the smell of charcoal, trying to relax her mind. Whispers from the embers tell her the premonition forecast by the east wind is on its way. What she doesn't know is how bad it is this time. Rico laughs at her visions, but that was what saved them five years ago. That's when the princess appeared in her dreams, told her what to do, and then they'd jumped worlds and ended up here. Even Wanita came with them.

She thinks about Rico, their life together for a decade in their last world – a place of two suns and seven moons. They'd met at a camel auction and ten years later his finger had itched. He'd tried to leave without her, but the ring wouldn't let him go, not without his soulmate. That's when everything came out. His princess; the emperor; Rico's punishment for sins in a previous life. They'd tried to escape across a desert but had been caught. Without the princess, it would have been the end, and they'd never have found themselves living this new existence.

But now it's happening again.

She pulls her dressing gown tight and concentrates on the fire. A crackle hisses back at her.

'I'm here,' whispers a man's voice from the flames.

She leans closer to the hearth. Heat warms her cheeks. 'Who are you?'

'You know who I am. What do you really know about your soulmate?'

She glances at the screen door. He should be back already, but the rain has probably slowed him down. He'll be frustrated, wanting to get home to join her in bed; not want to accept what's happening; not want to think about moving on. Soulmate. She lets the word settle. If the ring had worked, he'd have left her last time. How much does she know about him? His princess had forgiven his sins. He'd never said any more and she'd not asked, not wanted to know. It couldn't be that bad. They'd been together for long enough now.

'Take my gift. It'll tell you everything. Don't let my daughter brainwash you.' The voice again.

One of the logs falls forward, something drops through the bars of the basket and clatters against the brass fender. She goes to pick it up but stops herself. 'I don't understand.'

'It's perfectly safe. We'll talk later.'

The logs hiss and there's a puff of smoke at the back of the grate.

Mary picks up a smouldering memory stick.

VII

Drizzle becomes bouncing downpour, and Rico struggles to keep his footing on the downward slope leading to the farmhouse, his trainers sliding on the grassy bank. The rain has soddened his T-shirt and shorts, but he's more worried by the growing itch underneath the ring. A gift from his princess, her implanted DNA in the diamonds acting as an early warning device, allowing him with a single kiss to jump worlds, to stay free from the emperor and the fearsome Jinga.

He shudders at the memory of how close they'd come to being caught; the only occasion the ring had failed him. Five years ago, escaping by the skin of their teeth, the ring demanding Mary and his lips to activate, but he knew the chase wasn't over. The emperor wouldn't give up his pursuit of his daughter's champion. He thinks about his princess, how she'd given him another shot at life. He can never repay the debt. Without her, he would never have met Mary.

He reaches the porch steps, rain streaming down his face, and rips open the screen door. Mary is sitting by the fireplace, seemingly mesmerised by the yellow and blue flames being pulled up the chimney. She breaks her trance and looks at him. 'It's happening again.'

Rico rushes over and kneels in front of her.

'I fell asleep and—'

He puts a finger to her lips. 'I thought you'd be in bed.'

'The rain woke me.'

Hailstones pelt the windows. They look at each other. He twists the ring, scratches the itch.

'You feel them too,' she says.

'It's nothing. Sweat from running.'

Mary stands, her silk dressing gown gaping, giving Rico a brief glimpse of her thigh. His groin stirs. 'Where are you going?'

'To get dressed and check Wanita. We might need her.'

'She's fine. She'll be under cover.'

'I need to feed the dogs, sort out someone to look after them. We can't ignore the signs. Aren't you worried?'

'There's nothing to worry about. The storm will pass.'

She grabs his arms. 'I feel them, Rico.'

VIII

The teller sisters step back from the loom and look towards their princess, revealing a new scene. Mary and Rico in a bedroom, hurriedly pulling clothes from a wardrobe; Rico tugging on jeans and drying himself with a towel at the same time.

'There's something different about the girl,' says Livia, easing into her throne.

'You think your father has spoken to her?' says Sebastian.

'I know he has.'

A man wearing a brown cassock enters the room and walks over to them. He bows and kneels. 'Your Majesty.'

'No need to bow, Bernard,' says Livia, pulling him to his feet. 'Give me your advice.'

He walks over to the loom and studies the woven images. 'The emperor didn't expect changes.'

'I'm trying to make gods more compassionate. Is it wrong to show mercy?'

'Mercy for one man could crack a culture. Maybe that's why Octavius pursues Rico.'

'I can't let Octavius dictate or my whole reign will be in jeopardy.'

'Your champion and his soulmate have the ring. Is that not enough?'

She shakes her head. 'It's only a matter of time before they're caught. The Jinga get better at tracking their world shifts.'

'Which is why you need a distraction, another prey.'

'Will my plan work?'

'Possibly. But why would anyone take such a role? They're bound to get caught.'

'I'll give him no choice.'

IX

Fats treads carefully and follows the albino in silence up a spiral staircase, passing white stone walls with signs of green mould, the temperature getting colder the higher they climb. He wants to ask questions, but something tells him to keep quiet until he knows what's going on.

They reach a landing and a large oak door with a brass handle halfway up. Sebastian pushes the door open and gestures for Fats to go ahead of him. 'After you.'

He steps into the room and gasps.

Glass walls, ceiling and floor, a grandstand view of the outside and a vista he's only ever seen in films. Orbiting planets of different sizes, stars stretching to the beginning of time and, exactly level with the tower, the unmistakeable blue marble view of Earth revolving round its fire pit of a sun. So close, he feels like he could reach out the window and touch it.

'Quite something, isn't it?'

He looks towards the direction of the voice. A woman, long black hair, pinstripe suit, red pixie boots, sitting on a platinum throne. He shakes his head as the woman's image pulsates in and out of the chair, in line with a steady heartbeat. She's surrounded by a silver halo, which glows and reflects off her translucent face. 'This can't be real.'

'Maybe it isn't,' says the woman. 'You know you're dead?'

Fats nods.

'Some humans struggle with that. Do you want to know what happens next?'

He nods again, conscious of not saying anything, but it doesn't feel like he has permission. He forces himself to push out a few words. 'I can't believe I'm here,' he says, looking again at the images of space beyond the glass.

'You're on top of the world. It's the best view I have of my empire.'

'Your empire?'

'That's right.'

'You're God?'

'If you like,' she says, laughing. 'What's the matter? Not what you expected?'

He falls into silence again, wanting to say no, closely followed by, what the fuck. He looks towards Sebastian and then back at the woman. She suddenly seems much taller. 'Explain the options to him,' she says.

'Three possibilities,' says the albino. 'Destruction. Rebirth. Nirvana.'

'Nirvana?'

'Nice try. But with your track record, there's only two. Destruction is obvious. Rebirth is complicated.'

'I don't understand.'

'Another shot at life. Different person, different circumstances, but, well, let's face it, your soul should be liquidised. Lucky for you, the princess is offering something else.'

Fats faces the woman, who stares at Earth, looking as though she's not paying any attention. She pulls a cloth from her coat pocket, reaches down and rubs at a scuff mark on one of her boots. *What the fuck is going on here?* He tries to clear his head, tells himself not to be overwhelmed by the view, the occasion. Death could come at any time in his profession, which made it wise not to think about it too much, just stay in the moment. Even so, this isn't what he expected. It sounds like there's a deal, a shot at redemption. But there must be a price. There's always a price.

'Are you listening?' says Sebastian.

'You want me to do something.'

'Very perceptive,' says the woman, smiling.

'Not really. Everybody wants something, don't they, lady?'

Sebastian walks over and punches him in the face.

'Fucking hell,' says Fats, raising a hand to his nose, blood dribbling through his fingers.

'Your Highness,' says Sebastian. 'That's how you address the princess.'

'You're not on the street now,' says the woman. 'I'm thinking of offering you a way out, another chance, but I could just as easily find a replacement. There are thousands, millions of options. You, at the moment, are in the lucky seat, but if you don't—'

'No. I mean, yes. I'm sorry. It's just all come… I'm still getting my head round what's happening.'

Sebastian looks at Livia.

She waves her hand. 'Let him have his chance.'

X

Emperor Octavius walks away from the plasma pool in the middle of his starship's glass floor. He stares out the window, hands behind his back, and watches a purple dust planet glide by. For a moment, his mind wanders and remembers the day everything changed. Watched by his daughter, Livia, he played cards with his brother, Wrath. A straight flush beats four kings. How he regrets that hand. His empress, Helena, sucked back to the underworld to repay the debt, her time in the heavens over. Fate decided by the shuffle of a pack.

Although still a child, Livia's darted glares from that moment told him he would never be forgiven. She dares not risk his temper by saying anything, but he knows how she feels. He misses her, but things can never be the same. He thinks about her childhood, cloud surfing, chasing moons, him letting her win the race. All gone now. He tries to be lenient, give her some freedom to rule while he quests across galaxies, but he can't let her ruin his empire. And then, there's the human. The game. Putting her precious champion's life on the line is his way of teaching her strategy. She bettered him last time, but one-off victories are to be expected with the gene pool he's passed on. It can't happen again. That will give her too much strength and embolden his enemies. 'Captain,' he snaps. 'Give me an update.'

A heavily muscled man goose-steps through the fog circling the deck. He has a hoop ring through his nose and wears a warrior's skirt and ankle-length Roman caligae over bare feet and legs. Buffed, tanned leather panels adorn the top half of his body, suction clinging to every part of his torso, showing every sinew. 'Your Majesty,' he says, after coming to a halt and clicking his heels. 'Everything is ready. The Jinga will march when the order is issued.'

Octavius looks him up and down. 'And we're keeping a check on the whereabouts of the humans?'

'We track them through the ring. Do you want us to start the pursuit?'

'Not yet. I want to see how the woman reacts.'

'We can—'

'I said, not yet. I don't want any mistakes. My shield is holding?'

'It is. You can talk freely to the woman as long as she's alone.'

'Livia must be kept in the dark for as long as possible.'

'The ring is a worry, sir.'

'Relax,' says Octavius. 'One of the soulmates doubts her love, and the ring will fail while that is the case. Livia's champion will not leave without her. We'll see what she does when she finds out the truth about him.'

'Yes, sir,' says the captain, clicking his heels again.

'And what of Livia's plans to change my empire?'

'Blocked so far.'

'You look puzzled, Captain.'

'It's not my place to question, but why not return home, put an end to your daughter's reign and restore the status quo?'

'I agreed an aeon, and it'll do my enemies good to experience life without me. Anyway, I'm comforted by your reassurance we'll be informed of every move in my absence. Is that not the case?'

'Our spies have infiltrated every level.'

'There we are, then. Nothing to worry about, apart from these humans.' He reaches out and touches the glass. 'Are you married?'

'No, sir. My work—'

'Yes, quite right. And what's your view on soulmates?'

The captain looks at the floor, making the emperor smile.

'I'll take your silence as respect. You can breathe.'

'Thank you, sir. Will there be anything else?'

Octavius waves a dismissive hand and stares again out the window. Two suns face each other on opposite sides of space, like celestial gods preparing their chariots for a wartime advance. Next to them, a cluster of dusty, icy comets chase around diamond-encrusted stars; all of it framed by an orbiting carpet of ocean-blue and flame-red planets. 'Let us see how good you are, my daughter.'

XI

Paloma, the eldest of the teller sisters, stops weaving and steps back from the loom. *This game,* she thinks, *where will it end?* Her eyes track across the tapestry, scanning the quality of each weft and warp, and then she stops and peers at one of the scenes. It can't be. 'You need to see this.'

Sini pushes herself slowly to her feet from her stool in front of the spinning wheel, rubbing her knees and back as she hobbles across the glass floor. 'What is it? Disturbing my work. You know my bones jar getting up. You'll blame me if the wool isn't ready for you to weave.'

'Look,' says Paloma, 'in the corner of that field.'

They stand side by side and stare at the woven image.

'You must have weaved it,' says Sini.

'I did no such thing. It just appeared.'

'Impossible. We decide the fates.'

'Only if gods allow.'

'But they never interfere with our gift.'

A door opens at the far end of the atrium and Livia strides into the room, closely followed by Sebastian. 'What are you doing?' she says, walking towards them. 'Why aren't you working?'

'There's something new,' says Paloma. 'Something we didn't create.'

Livia follows their gaze and looks at the tapestry.

Sebastian steps to her side. 'What is it?'

'Octavius has woven his own fate. It's the woman, on her own in the barn, looking at something. Are we still not able to see her through the pool?'

'Your father shields her. We can only see her when she's with your champion.'

'We must know what she's doing.'

'Why would the emperor tell us his actions by weaving the woman's face? It doesn't make sense.'

'A taunt. A reminder of his power.'

'We could put eyes on the planet. Visit the woman in person.'

'The gangster? Not yet. What were you working on when you noticed this image?'

Paloma steps back to the loom and traces a gnarled forefinger round a woollen scene. She looks at her sister as though she's about to say something, but Sini shakes her head, and they stay silent.

'The smoke humans,' says Livia. 'They'll do anything to have their bodies restored.'

Sebastian gives her an anxious look. 'Can you trust them? With their history.'

'No one knows their past or why Octavius punished them, but the fates say they're part of the story. Maybe we can use them for this job. Bring them to me at once. Wait. Where is my champion now?'

Sebastian walks over to the plasma pool, hot liquid popping away on the glass floor, and runs his hand across the surface. An image of Rico, sitting at a table in the farmhouse kitchen. 'He looks sad.'

'Confused,' says Livia. 'He's wondering about Mary. So am I.'

XII

Four smoke humans waft in front of the platinum throne, trying to keep their gaseous forms as still as possible. It's not easy. Their bodies react to the slightest draught creeping through the atrium, but they're trying to give an air of respect towards the princess. It's been a long time since they were in this room, back when their presence was welcome. All of that changed when the emperor altered their fates. If only they could say what they wanted, try to restore their previous status, but that would bring out more of Octavius's fury. Being here again by invite gives them hope of resolution, and they're determined not to let it go to waste. They've been told to keep silent until given permission to speak but can't resist whispering amongst themselves.

'This could be it, escape…'

'Do you think we'll get another chance?'

'Why else would they grant an audience after ignoring us for so long?'

Sebastian watches from the back of the room as Livia takes her seat. He tries to calculate if this is a good idea. No one is saying why the emperor removed the bodies of these humans. All memory of them has been banished. The puzzle is why they exist in smoke form instead of being destroyed. Rumour has them doing everything from buggering the empress to stealing the crown jewels, but it's the emperor's leniency that confuses Sebastian. They must have committed a heinous crime to be dissolved but still be needed for some reason.

'Which of you is spokesperson?' says Livia.

Three of the smoke humans look towards the fourth.

She tries to anchor her vision on the man's features – a body blurring to separate parts through plumes of interlocking smoke; Afro hair plonked on his head like a crown. 'Your name.'

'Jethro, Your Highness. I speak for us.'

'I want you to do something for me. Just you, but if you're successful, I'll reward all of you.'

'Reward in what way?'

'I'm assuming you'd like to be restored, given another chance.'

Jethro's face flushes with excitement. His brothers dance round him.

'But I'll extinguish you if you fail.'

She waits for a reaction, expects remorse, even a

plea to be saved, but, through the ash-grey outline of Jethro's head, she sees a row of battered yellow teeth and realises the smoke human is smiling. And then she hears laughter from the other smoke humans.

'Silence,' says Sebastian, stepping forward.

The laughter stops.

'You find this funny?' says Livia.

'No,' says Jethro. 'It's just, well, to be honest, after so long in this form, being extinguished is not a punishment. Either option would be a mercy. And, in any case, the emperor might need us.'

'Need you? Why would the emperor of gods need four humans?'

The brothers look at each other. 'He's kept us for this long,' says Jethro.

'What did you do to deserve this punishment?'

He smiles again.

She looks at Sebastian and then at the image on the loom.

The sisters nod.

'The fate has been woven,' says Livia, sitting back on her throne. 'Tell him what to do.'

XIII

Bernard touches a narrow scar on his right cheek – a heated poker gift from his father. It reminds him to bite his lip whenever emotions threaten to overwhelm – a lesson he's zealously self-inflicted throughout life, with any feelings repressed, kept at bay. Cigarettes are his favourite. Nothing serious. A sizzle to singe the hair on his forearms and thighs. Enough to keep him on track.

Done for today, he unrolls his sleeve, covers his arm, dampens the cigarette in a tin ashtray and thinks about the princess. She deserves better, but everyone has to survive, and the last time he checked, no one watches his back. He eases into a leather wing chair and looks round the glass attic that has been his home forever. It always surprises him in these moments of reflection how little he has acquired over the years, but that's been his choice. A table, chair, some candles, a bookcase with assorted, dusty hardbacks never read, and a bed. It's enough. Clutter bogs you down. It's much the same with people. That's what he believes. He's hardly got anything by getting too involved. People expect things. Best to stay distant. Look after number one.

He picks up his mug, the one covered in sunflowers, and drains the remains of his coffee, registering the bitter, warm caffeine slide down his throat. That done, he puts the mug back on the table, sits up, brings his hands together in front of his mouth and taps his lips with his fingers, in contemplation mode. 'Growler,' he bellows.

'Yes, Master,' comes a voice from the far corner of the room.

'You have my telescope?'

A black fur ball with stunted legs and arms hops over to the chair. 'Here you are, Master.'

He looks down at his pet cosmic urchin, Growler's watery seal eyes blinking up at him as he hands over the telescope. 'I need to know what the fates have in store. Any news from the network?'

'Nothing, Master. Except what you know already from the princess.'

'And the emperor? What are his plans?'

'No one knows.'

'Do we still have Jinga loyal to the cause?'

'We do, but they're reluctant—'

'Reluctant. We need to find out what's going on.'

More blinks from Growler. 'The princess has recruited.'

'The ally. I know about him. She seeks a distraction.'

'Not just him. She summons the smoke humans to spy for her.'

Bernard unfurls the telescope and points it towards a distant galaxy. *Families,* he thinks. *They're always guaranteed to turn on each other.* He looks again at the urchin. 'Something is about to change, my wide-eyed friend.'

XIV

A lichen-covered cave halfway up a hillside, a view of the valley below, has been home for four smoke humans since the emperor removed their solid form. Here they sit, night after night, huddled round an eternal campfire, their smoke bodies wafting in the air, only leaving when summoned by gods to make their daily penance. Each morning, they perch cross-legged in the middle of a lake, humming their prayers, ribbons of fog surrounding them, asking for forgiveness, shifting their pleas through the vocal ranges, bass, baritone, tenor, hitting soprano and throwing their hands skywards, black eyes staring expectantly towards the heavens. Lost souls waiting for a new life. No response for so many years, but now one of their number has been chosen, called away on a mission for the princess.

The remaining brothers bob in front of the fire, muttering.

'I can't believe the fates have weaved us into their tapestry.'

'I'd almost given up hope.'

'Jethro is lucky to get out.'

Embers crackle. Wind whispers through their smoky bodies, making them shimmy a ghostly dance, arms and legs looking as though they're on strings controlled by a puppet master. Their faces, eyes, noses, mouths fade in and out of view, with the identical twins twisting in and out of each other's form, only distinguishable by Thomas's goatee and Alfie's lip and nose studs – red hearts with an arrow splitting their centre. Next to them, Michael, the third brother, who has a perfectly round, completely shaven head. All wear brown cassocks – another penance handed down by the emperor.

Thomas holds his smoky hands towards the fire and rubs them together – a habit he's kept from his solid days. 'The princess looked worried.'

'She should be,' says Alfie, pulling at his foggy lip stud with his gaseous fingers – another twitch kept from life. 'She's on trial, and the emperor isn't known for tolerance. I don't understand why he gave her power in the first place.'

'A game,' says Michael. 'He likes the jeopardy. Look what happened to Helena.'

'You were in charge of the cards.' A voice from the back of the cave.

'I wondered how long it would take for you to show up,' says Michael.

Bernard steps from the shadows and crouches in front of the fire.

The smoke humans look at each other and then glare at him.

'I'm starting to feel unwelcome,' he says.

'What do you want?' says Michael.

'Am I not allowed to visit my brothers? Thomas, unsealed any cards lately? Michael, the shuffler. Alfie, restacking supremo. Only Jethro, the dealer, is missing.'

'We're not brothers. We share a father, and you're the only bastard.'

'Still blaming me for your incompetence, Michael?'

'We were framed, and your mother was a whore. That doesn't make you family.'

'Perhaps I should tell the princess who you are, about your lack of care for Helena.'

'The emperor wiped her memory of us. Why would she believe you?'

'I'm the only kin she has.'

'God help her. We trusted you, and look how that worked out.'

'You were careless, left yourself vulnerable. At least you're still alive.'

'This is no life—'

'Can you help us?' says Thomas.

'We can help each other,' says Bernard.

'The price,' says Michael. 'What's the price?'

'Information. Nothing more. I want to know what Jethro sees.'

'Does your princess know you go behind her back?'

'I protect her.'

Michael sucks his lips and looks at the twins.

'We need him,' says Alfie. 'What choice do we have?'

'Jethro will never agree.'

'You'll never know unless you ask him,' says Bernard.

XV

A draught of icy air grabs Fats' breath as he drops off the train.

He's glad of his snuggly donkey jacket, woollen hat, scarf and gloves. He lights a cigarette, blows smoke at the tin roof and looks along the wind tunnel platform, patting his pocket to check the map is still there and the credit card the princess gave him for expenses. She's watching. He knows that. But for now, he has to do nothing. Just be ready when she calls.

Dead.

It feels weird because he's not. He's walking round the same town, breathing the same air, but he knows he's on licence. Like a lifer, he can get called back any time to face the consequences. A shiver runs down his back. The things he's seen. Moons, stars and Earth up close, a realisation of being a speck of dust in God's empire. He's still not sure what she is, the princess. And that albino. The way he'd said destruction, like it was a favourite sport.

He pushes the thought from his mind. A second chance. All he has to do is not fuck it up. Keep the map safe and wait to be contacted, that's what she'd said. Easy. And meantime, he just has to keep himself out of trouble.

A train pulls in at the next platform. A station announcer bangs out a garbled message over the Tannoy.

Fats takes another drag of his fag. And that's when he sees him, limping, large as bloody life, towards the exit.

Ricky No Toes.

A smog falls in Fats' head as he watches Ricky's back walk away from him. A gravel car park; a boot in the ribs; 'I'm going to enjoy hearing your screams'; Rottweilers ripping clumps from his flesh; the posse cheering and laughing from the stands of the swimming pool.

Throwing the cigarette butt to the concrete floor, he grinds it to death under the heel of his Doc Marten and follows Ricky towards the street.

XVI

Mary sits on the barn floor, opens a laptop and fetches the memory stick from her cotton dress pocket. Gertie, a white owl they found half dead in the bushes when they first arrived, hoots at her from the eaves and blinks a dreamy hello.

The owl is one part of Mary's waif and stray menagerie. A family of misfits. Gertie, Wanita, the dogs and, she smiles at the thought, a Rico. She brushes her red hair from her eyes and thinks about the day they met. A camel auction, her bidding on a twenty-year-old cow who'd been condemned to death and put up for meat trade sale. Rico must have thought she was mad as she stood on a five-bar gate, chewing a piece of straw, Stetson pulled low over her face, waving her arms and snarling her bids, staring down the butcher, her only competitor. 'What'll you call her?' Rico had asked as she'd collected her reward.

'Wanita. After my Hawaiian grandmother.' The next thing she knew they were trundling back to the ranch in her father's bronco, Wanita tied to the rear bumper, lolloping along the sand, and Rico sat in the passenger seat, clutching a bottle of tequila.

Fifteen years later, here they were, and she still doesn't know who he is.

Rico's sins, being pursued across galaxies by a father and protected by a princess who'd given him a ring. She'd accepted it all, but now the emperor, the one chasing Rico, comes to her dreams and pricks her curiosity. What had he done? She rolls the memory stick over in her hand and looks at the computer. All she has to do…

'And will that help?'

Her head shoots up and she peers into the fug of a smoke bubble that fills the void in-between two beams. She makes out a shape. A man with stained teeth smiling at her. 'Who are you?' she says, nervously glancing at the barn door, checking there's a route of escape.

'Jethro. The princess sent me.'

She pushes the memory stick back in her pocket and stands up. The smoke reminds her of clouds shapeshifting across the sky, the ones she tracked and talked to as a child. Ever changing. No two moments the same. The only thing that stays constant is Jethro's warm smile.

The fug drifts closer. 'Do you think knowing about his past will help?'

Mary steps back, thinks about calling for Rico but changes her mind when Jethro smiles again. 'It might. I've always wondered—'

'You love everything you know about him. Is that not enough?'

Rico's face – azure-blue eyes, chipped front tooth, celestial nose turned up at the end – and then there's his kindness, his touch…

'Sounds like everything you need.'

She shakes her head. The smoke human reading her thoughts makes her shudder. 'Are you part of this chase?'

'The princess is trying to help.'

'By stopping me looking at a memory stick?'

'The emperor confuses you, makes you doubt your love.'

'Is Rico's secret really that bad?'

Jethro moves back towards the beams. 'That form of Rico has gone. The Rico who lives today is the one you fell in love with. Remember the last fifteen years. You'll need to be strong together, if you're going to survive.'

'Then we are under threat. They've found us.'

'The princess will do what she can. And I'll help as much as I'm able.'

A wisp of wind through the eaves blows the smoke human out of existence.

Mary hears Wanita grunting from the paddock.

She reaches down, closes the laptop lid, puts it under her arm and hurries across the barn floor towards the door.

XVII

Livia pounds her trainer-shod feet on a treadmill, banging out a quick rhythm. She concentrates on the sound, wills herself to keep pace. She's never broken forty-five minutes, but today, on her 10K morning ritual, adrenalin fires her forward, her body feels good and… just keep going… She hits the stop button. 44:48 in red luminous digits beat out at her. She punches the air, grabs a towel from the back of the machine and mops her brow before taking a slug of water from a platinum flask.

'Well done, my darling.' A familiar voice drips from a purple orb, a truth sayer, levitating in front of her, soothing sparks of electric charge fizzing across its surface, a face with chocolate-brown eyes smiling through.

The first time she'd seen her mother's image and heard her voice coming from the orb she'd panicked, thought it some kind of trick played by her father or, even worse, a tease from Uncle Wrath, sent from hell. But now, for the most part, the orb brings her down from any rush of adrenalin. She has to be careful, though. It also revives memories of the card game and the last time she'd seen her mother alive, being dragged to hell by Beelzebub.

She takes another drink and looks round the gym, an extension of her private space just below the atrium. Everything to keep her part-human body in peak condition, but the cardio machines are her favourite. Weights build strength, but racing her heart on the treadmill, bike and skier frees her mind, dissolves the stress of wearing a ruler of the afterlife mask. And then there's the orb – a spiritual gift from Octavius after he lost his gamble with Wrath – specially made on the planet Aletheia, sprinkled with Helena's DNA – forged by ancients to answer any question with the truth. 'It can never replace her,' he'd said, expecting gratitude, but she'd cursed him, pushed his present away, only changing her mind when he'd left it in her quarters before going on his quest.

'He still doesn't know we talk,' says the orb, purple light pulsing as it speaks.

Livia wipes her forehead. 'I'm glad you're here.'

'Your mother will return. I can feel—'

'Is that a truth?'

Silence.

A pattern from the orb of late, expressing feelings rather than fact, which Livia puts down to a clumsy attempt to try and be of comfort. She realises it can only give the truth if it knows the answer, but she wishes it would just say, 'I don't know.'

'Talk about something else,' she snaps.

The orb blinks twice. 'You're getting fitter.'

'The ecclesia thinks I'm foolish with my exercise.'

'What do they know about human ways?'

She feels her blood pressure rise at the thought of the ecclesia. Four gods and a human left by Octavius to guide and protect but also to keep her changes in check. With them, even Octavius must plan his route carefully. She kicks off her trainers and socks, unrolls a yoga mat across the gym floor, lies down and stares at the ceiling. This place, her comfort zone where no one else is allowed, built by Octavius to feed Livia's need for solitude, sanctuary, whatever you want to call it. A place of her own.

'He's a kind soul. But a god, consumed with arrogance and pride.'

'I don't want to think about him.'

A blink from the orb releases the fragile, honey-tuned voice of Gurrumul, a blind aboriginal singer. A gift from her mother, it always eases her into relaxation, takes her to a ghostly realm, somewhere clean, untouched. She doesn't understand a word, but the haunting lyrics caress her spirit – drag a cleansing balm through her body. She closes her eyes, spreads her arms, hands palm down against the floor – the closest she can get to a connection with Earth.

The melting sound fills the room, but then, something else comes crashing through her protective walls, forcing her to grip the floor, suppress her panic. She fights the urge to open her eyes, concentrates on the music, which the orb blinks louder, but the image is still there in her head. A twitching antenna sniffing the air; bulging eyes; transparent bat wings flapping furiously to keep it hovering over marshy ground. *Go away. Go away.*

Gurrumul's voice increases in volume; Beelzebub twitches; his face contorts as she pushes the aboriginal singer's caress towards the demon, who screams as the earth sucks him from existence with a pop, like quicksand on speed.

She draws deep breaths, feels her heart rate settle and, finally, another image. Night-time. She's sitting on a white sand beach, a tide rolling into her thoughts. She stares at a full moon. Its beams make the ocean appear frozen silver. She drops her eyes to track a path of luminescent algae drifting across the surface of the water, like the stars have fallen from the sky. And then the algae dart backwards and forwards, backwards and forwards. She flashes her eyes left, right, left, right, to keep up with its pace. Slowly, it comes to a standstill, and she lies there keeping the moon and algae in view, burying herself in the sound of lapping waves.

Ten minutes later, the music fades to silence and she comes back into the room, opens her eyes and sits up on the mat.

'Refreshed?' blinks the orb.

'You were there. Walking on the beach in front of me, but he held my hand, stopped me from catching up with you.'

'He'd never do that. He loves you, despite what you think.'

'I called, but you carried on walking.'

'I didn't hear you.'

She jumps to her feet and rolls up the mat. 'I need to shower and change.'

'The pinstripe suit. Something else the ecclesia doesn't understand.'

'It keeps them on the back foot, gives me a chance to get a word in edgeways.'

'Even Athos?'

A blush fills her cheeks, and she looks away. 'He doesn't seem to mind.'

'He doesn't mind. Not one iota. And that is a truth.'

The orb falls silent as Livia gives it one final glance before walking away to her bedroom.

*

Back in the atrium, Livia rubs Paloma's knotty shoulders as she stands behind her and watches her weave. The teller sisters have been around all her life, but she's never thought to ask their story and where they come from and never questioned what they are or what they do. Her mother trusted them, and so does she, and, for most gods, future paths can't exist unless they've been foretold by the fates.

Paloma turns and smiles. 'Your mother would be proud of you.'

Sini, sitting behind them on her spinning stool, nods her agreement.

'You served her well,' says Livia.

'She may return,' says Paloma, without taking her gaze off the loom.

Tears flood Livia's eyes, but she blinks them away. She sees her mother's image in her mind. Wavy panther-black hair cascading to her waist; Livia sitting on her lap, looking up at her, listening to her stories of pirates and their treasure-hunting escapades across high seas. She senses the touch of soft hands stroking her face, big hugs keeping her safe. Octavius worshipped his human wife, his soulmate, fell in love the moment he saw her reflection in a lake from his cloud chariot, seduced her as she walked alongside the water, drawing her into his spell disguised as a white dove, revealing himself at the last minute, when it was too late to escape his embrace. Her mother told the story over and over, saw it as a compliment that she'd been chosen. 'And it gave me you, my darling.' But then he'd got careless, used his empress as a gambling chip… 'No,' she says, forcing herself to concentrate on the tapestry. 'She's gone forever.'

The fates look at each other.

Livia reaches out and traces her finger round the weaved image of Mary. 'The woman is with my champion?'

'She is,' says Paloma.

'What news from the smoke human?'

Sebastian kneels by the plasma pool and draws his hand across the bubbling liquid. 'Your father has given the woman a memory stick with details of Rico's sins. She's not opened it yet.'

Livia sits back on her throne, looking thoughtful. 'Have they tried kissing the ring?'

'They seem unsure what to do.'

'If she has doubts about her love, the ring won't work. The gangster, where is he?'

Sebastian focusses again on the pool.

'Ah,' says Livia, looking at the image. 'We knew he'd get distracted.'

'Shall I bring him back?'

'Leave him. Let him carry out his chase. The next move is for Octavius. When he realises the woman resists, he'll send the Jinga, and the humans will try to jump worlds. We'll find out then if their love holds.'

'And if it doesn't?'

She nods at the teller sisters. 'That's when you'll forge a different path.'

XVIII

Octavius stands on his viewing platform contemplating what to do, fully conscious of his captain waiting for instructions. Hopes of a quick resolution to the game have been thrown back in his face, with the woman shunning the memory stick and leaving it unopened. He lets the disappointment settle. There's a whispering voice in his head telling him to concentrate on rebuilding his relationship with Livia, but, at the moment, the game is their only connection. If only he could think of a better way to get her and Helena back in his life. For now, there is no other option but to play out his emperor role.

He takes a deep breath and claps three times.

A gong sounds. An explosion. Smoke bursts from the walls.

Thud, thud, thud.

A circle of lights illuminates the stage.

Thud, thud, thud.

Two warriors storm into view, a Jinga trademark

hoop ring through their nostrils; buffalo hide vests pressing against sweaty torsos; bare legs dropping into thick-soled, hobnailed marching caligae secured to their ankles with leather thongs. With a final thud, they come to a standstill, heel click and salute. 'Your Majesty!'

'The woman ignores me,' says Octavius. 'My Jinga have their prey fixed in their minds?'

The captain steps forward from behind a central console. 'Yes, Emperor.'

Octavius claps again.

Two glass pods drop from the ceiling, each covering an individual warrior.

A second gong.

The pods shoot upwards, out of the ship, and fall towards the planet.

'I want no mistakes. The humans will be brought to me or destroyed. I don't care which.'

'We're tracking the ring,' says the captain, walking to his side. 'They won't escape.'

'Let Livia see the woman. It's only fair now the game starts.'

'The woman may still help us. She's retained the memory stick.'

'We can't rely on her. The smoke human refuels her love. I should have dealt with my wife's brothers more harshly—'

'You were grieving—'

'Don't presume to know my thoughts.'

The captain comes to attention and salutes. 'My apologies.'

Octavius glares at him for a few seconds more and then turns towards the window. 'I was too lenient. What news of Bernard? Does he still comfort Livia?'

'He does.'

'And plots against me, no doubt. For a human, he has many supporters.'

'Would you like him brought here? To account for himself.'

'Not yet,' says Octavius, turning and sitting on his throne. He picks up a goblet of wine and takes a sip. 'We'll capture the humans first.'

XIX

Mary lets the barn door slam behind her. She sees Rico in the paddock, brushing Wanita, the camel groaning contentedly and stretching her neck to browse on the leaves of a eucalyptus tree, saliva drooling through her lips as she chomps.

Rico puts his hand in the air and Mary waves back.

She's still not sure what she should be thinking, but whenever she sees Rico's gentleness with Wanita, her heart melts. She pats her pocket to check the memory stick is still there. Perhaps she'll burn it. The smoke human is right. What more does she need to know after fifteen years? The one thing she's sure of is they're in trouble again. The emperor will come soon. It's time to leave.

She strides over to the paddock.

'Are you okay?' says Rico, hugging her close.

Mary squeezes him into her body. 'Is your finger still itching?'

He gently pushes her away. 'It's nothing.'

'You know that's not true. I've seen them, Rico. In my dreams. We need to leave.'

'I'm sick of running.'

'We've no choice. I've messaged Jenny. Told her we're going away. She'll sort the dogs.'

Wanita farts.

Rico laughs. 'I suppose the camel's coming.'

She lifts his hand and rubs the ring round Wanita's slobbering lips. 'Her saliva will bring her. Now, we do this together.'

They kiss the diamonds.

Nothing.

They look at each other.

'Try again,' says Mary.

They kiss the ring once more.

Nothing.

'That can't be right,' says Rico, taking the ring off his finger and holding it up to the light. He inspects it for damage. It looks fine. He reaches in his pocket, pulls out a cleaning cloth, wipes the ring inside and out and pushes it back on his finger. Mary rubs it round Wanita's lips again and they kiss the diamonds one more time.

Nothing.

She sees the fear in Rico's face, which starts anxiety waves rolling in her stomach. Without the ring, they're lost. 'Is this what happened last time? When the ring needed both our lips.'

'Exactly the same, but that was because we fell in love, and it wouldn't let one of us go without the other.'

'And now it's stopped working.'

'Perhaps it's because we don't need to leave. We're not being chased.'

'I've told you. They've come to me. We're in danger.'

He looks up into the hills. His finger itches, but everything else seems okay. No Jinga shadows; no warrior marching towards them with an ultimatum. The rain clouds have moved away. There's even a glint of blue sky and a flash of sun peeping over the top of the woods. The only thing he hears is birdsong and Wanita chomping. And yet Mary seems certain. Her visions aren't always right, but his itching finger and the ring not working... 'Who's come to you? Was it the princess?'

'No,' says Mary, touching her pocket again and checking the memory stick. She thinks about the emperor visiting her dreams, talking to her through the fire, what he said about Rico's sins. She can't say any of that to Rico. Not yet. 'A messenger. She sent someone to warn us.'

'I don't understand.'

'You're going to laugh, but it's... well, it's a smoke human.'

'What?'

'He said he'd try and help us.'

'You're not making sense.'

'I'll show you,' she says, pulling him towards the barn.

XX

Fats has never really appreciated how fast Ricky No Toes can walk, but he's never chased him through the streets before. He guesses Ricky has adapted over the years since Jean got another of her gorillas to take an axe to his feet. Jean's justice after Ricky tried to leave, go straight. 'He'll not be walking away so quickly next time,' she'd told Fats one night in bed. *That's the problem with Jean,* thinks Fats. *Once you're in, there's no getting out.* And when she gets tired of you between the sheets, you become cannon fodder, ranking about three places below her precious Rottweilers. Fats wonders how much Ricky had to reduce his shoe size after the toes went in Jean's mincer. She did that while Ricky was still tied to a chair, made him watch the grinder. A nice treat for the dogs.

He hard blows as he keeps on Ricky's trail past Smith's, Woolworths, HMV. It feels strange but comforting to be back in the normal world after the weirdness of the afterlife. The only unsettling thing is a scream of revenge racing round his head. He wants it to be slow, lingering, but has no idea how he'll do it. It'll have to be hands-on, but Ricky is strong – a pumped-up bruiser. No toes make his balance wobbly, but that's about the only advantage Fats can think of. Perhaps Ricky will die of a heart attack when he sees him. Too quick. He needs to suffer.

A car horn honks as Fats dodges between the traffic, not having time to wait for the green man. He checks to see if Ricky looks back towards the sound, but his prey has his head down as he strides through town on a mission. Where's he going? And why isn't he driving? *It's not professional,* thinks Fats. Jean has a lot of enemies and working in her posse makes you a target. You learn early on never to walk anywhere, not to use public transport and to avoid being on your own. Three mantras to keep you alive.

He ducks into a doorway as Ricky stops in front of Debenhams and bends down to tie his shoelaces. Only he's not. Fats can see it's fake, a cover to check out the street. He calculates if Ricky has seen him, but he can't have. He's not looking behind. He's watching the apartments over the road.

And then Fats realises where he is.

Trailing Ricky at such a pace has made him lose his compass, but he knows now.

The entrance door to the apartments across the

road swings open and out steps a long-legged, mini-skirted blonde, holding the door behind her.

Ricky walks over and kisses her.

Gemma.

Jean's granddaughter.

Fats wants to laugh. Gemma's working her way round the gang, bringing on a sub. A form of flattery really, wanting what her grandmother has had. Not that Jean's objections are familial loyalty. She's pissed at being replaced by a younger model. Okay for her to do it, but the other way gets you gnawed by dogs. And that kick in the ribs Ricky gave him. Unnecessary. Even gangsters have their standards, and that kick was personal. It makes sense now. No man likes the bloke who makes him have sloppy seconds.

At least revenge is easy.

All he has to do is call Jean, disguised voice, but… shit. No mobile, just a credit card and loose change to get him through until the princess sends her summons. He'll have to do it the old-fashioned way. He looks back along the high street for a payphone.

A laugh forces its way through his lips, like an unexpected burp. He can't control it. Adrenalin oozes from him. A woman walks by holding the hands of two toddlers. She gives him a hard look and pulls the children closer. Fats puts a hand to his mouth, muffling the sound.

That payphone had better be working.

XXI

Mary pulls Rico into the barn, her head whirling. Part of her thinks she's the reason the ring isn't working – her doubts about Rico's past affecting the belief they're soulmates. The only test would be for Rico to kiss the ring alone, but then, if it works, she'll lose him forever. She points to the corner of the roof where the smoke human emerged. 'There. His name's Jethro.'

Rico follows her point.

Gertie hoots at them.

'There's nothing,' he says, putting his hand on Mary's arm.

'He said he'd try to help—'

'And I will.'

They look up at the plumes of smoke now floating in and out of the eaves, like ghosts playing an elaborate game of twister. Slowly, they merge, a face, eyes, nose, mouth and a nest of tight curly hair. 'Hello, Rico,' says Jethro, his stained teeth beaming a warm smile. 'I've heard a lot about you.'

Rico pulls Mary to his side. 'You're from the princess?'

'She wants to help,' says Jethro. 'The emperor has found your location.'

'And how do we know you're not a trick?'

'He can't be,' says Mary. 'Why would he warn us?'

'She's right, Rico.'

'I've learnt over centuries not to trust anyone but the princess. Why doesn't she come herself?'

'She keeps watch on her father. It's the only way to protect you.'

Rico looks at Mary. 'It could be a trap.'

'The emperor wouldn't send two messages,' she says.

'You've heard from him?'

'He visited my dreams, asked how much I really knew you.' She reaches into her pocket and pulls out the memory stick. 'He gave me this, said it would tell me about your sins.'

'Have you—'

She shakes her head. 'Jethro asked me what benefit it would bring. So, you see, he can't be a trick.'

'I'm not that person now, Mary.'

'I know.'

'But you have doubts. That might be why the ring has stopped working.'

Jethro coughs. 'There is another way. The princess has found you an ally.'

XXII

Bernard ponders Earth through his monastic room's glass window.

He's not set foot on home soil since the emperor awarded him immortality for revealing the cause of a lost card game. That was an eternity ago, and he misses the cobbled streets and graveyards of his childhood domain; the hours spent checking out the dead; reading their tombstone epitaphs; gauging from their start and end dates whether they'd had a decent existence; trying to work out where their souls had gone, if their spirits existed as ghosts and where they might appear. But that was before his elevation stripped away romance and wonderment – made life after death nothing more than ordinary.

In his mind, he sees a little boy hiding with corpses – a sad target for the whole world but a better option than risking the rage of his father or the indifference and pity of his siblings. A cuckoo in the nest. That's how he felt – a by-product of an illicit affair that surged his father's guilt every time he saw his bastard son in the house. He shrugs. All different now, ever since he grassed up his half-brothers. No guilt. Someone had to be accountable, and they'd placed themselves in jeopardy by taking on such high-profile roles. Brothers. They hate it when he reminds them of their shared blood. Their gamble might have brought them riches, but Wrath walking away with the spoils changed everything. How they'd despise him if they knew what he'd done. The dealer worries him the most. Clever Jethro sees through pretence, but he's heard nothing for decades, which settles his anxiety.

He concentrates again on Earth's land masses, oceans and swirls of clouds drifting lazily by. Transfixed as always by the blue surface, he thinks about his mother; wonders for the billionth time who she was, where she is now. He guesses he'll never know. Not that it matters. He found a way to survive. A fixed game of cards shuffled his destiny – something he pounced on like a lion hunting a gazelle. Since then, he's played a perfect ten with the ecclesia, taking no definite view, placing himself in a position of influence with all sides. Now is not the time to let the advantage leak. He must keep his nerve and find out what the dealer is doing.

'Growler,' he bellows.

The black fur ball wakes with a start in the corner

of the room, jumps up and hops over to stand in front of the leather wing chair. 'Yes, Master.'

'Is there anything to report?'

'Nothing. Our sources seem ignorant.'

'Then our best bet is the smoke humans. They know I have influence and have agreed to let you sit in their cave as my envoy. You need to be watchful, let me know immediately Jethro makes contact. Say nothing. We need to keep our neutrality. Do you understand?'

Growler blinks and hops towards the door.

XXIII

Livia closes her eyes and feels herself break free of tension with each of Sini's brush strokes. She hears her mother's sing-song voice in her head, purring the lyrics of Eddi Reader's 'The Girl Who Fell in Love with the Moon'. A playlist of human songs – a bequest to the heavens – but this one belongs to her. A whisper from her mother. 'It's you, my darling. Never lose your wonder.' She taps her foot as the lyrics and rhythm consume her. All she has to do is imagine a sky, any sky, and, with this song, her mother's gift of joy, it transports her to a world of magic and dreams.

'You have lovely hair,' says Sini.

'A gene present,' says Paloma, still weaving away at the loom.

Sini brushes from the top of Livia's head to just beyond her waist. 'It's so shiny. I can see my face.'

'Mother calmed my childhood tantrums with brushing.'

'Nonsense. You were a beautiful child. Running

through the orchard playing hide-and-seek. I remember once we thought you were lost, but the empress sensed you hiding in the bushes. A sixth sense only a human mother possesses. Your father should not—'

'Enough,' says Livia, closing down her mind music, opening her eyes and holding up her hand. She stands and walks over to the loom. 'What is happening with my champion?'

Sini gives her sister a nervous glance and sheepishly hurries back to her stool to resume her spinning of yarn. Paloma returns the look, stops weaving and steps back to give her princess a better view.

'The smoke human has done well,' says Livia. 'He's brought Rico and his girl back on track. At least now they understand the urgency.'

'But the ring still fails them,' says Sebastian, walking to her side. 'Which means we need the gangster.'

Livia shifts her gaze to another part of the tapestry. 'He seems to have completed his chase.'

'Shall I call him in?'

'We'll join him. A change of scenery will do me good.'

'You mean—'

'Exactly that, Sebastian. We're not wedded to this room.'

XXIV

Fats takes a sip of Pernod crème de menthe. 'Perfect. Just as I remember it.'

'You're sure that's what you want,' says the barman, pulling a face as Fats gulps a long slug of the green drink. 'Isn't it a bit like drinking toothpaste?'

'Reminds me of a girl I once knew. We used to drink these until our legs wobbled.'

'Lost love, eh. That explains it.'

'I'll have another,' says Fats, emptying the glass.

'Whatever you want, buddy.'

Fats turns on the bar stool and looks around. The guy who owns this place must be a football fan because a couple of the walls are covered in nicely embroidered, satin flags – Barcelona, Real Madrid, Bayern Munich, Juventus. No English clubs. Maybe that's deliberate in an English bar, nothing for the punters to fight over. Not that there are many of those. A man and woman snuggling close in one of the booths – Fats deduces an affair, too touchy-feely to be married; a few stools down from him there's a woman on her own, punching furiously into a laptop, trying too hard with make-up. She smiles at Fats. He looks away. At the far end of the bar, an old man nurses half a pint of lager. Fats guesses he used to come in here before it became posh, probably sat at the same table in a sticky-carpet working man's pub.

'Your drink, buddy.'

'Eh,' says Fats, going to pick up the glass and finding it empty. He looks at the barman.

Sebastian's pink eyes drill into him. 'Time to rock and roll, my friend.'

The roof and walls of the bar fall away, and Fats finds himself standing in a field with the albino at his side. 'The princess?' he asks.

'Right in front of you,' says Sebastian, nodding towards the far end of the glade.

Livia waves at him from underneath a eucalyptus tree. She's leaning against its gnarled trunk, rubbing one of its leaves. 'I see you've been enjoying yourself. The chase was a bit naughty.'

Sebastian squeezes Fats' arm, encouraging him to walk forward.

They fall in step and come to a standstill in front of her.

'Don't worry,' she says. 'I expected it. You'll be pleased to know your call was successful. Mr No Toes did not survive.'

He looks anxiously around the field.

Sebastian laughs. 'He's not here, buddy. Like we said before, you've been chosen.'

'You still have the map?' says Livia.

'Yes, Your Highness,' says Fats, feeling a prod in his back from the albino. 'I still have the map.'

'Good. Then Sebastian will go over your instructions one more time. And no more distractions. I'll be watching.'

XXV

Rico throws a saddlebag across Wanita's back and starts loading the supplies Mary has dragged from the farmhouse and piled at his side. Blankets, hydration packs, tins of beans. He stops and strokes the camel's head. She chews her lip, a disinterested look smearing her face.

'Found it,' shouts Mary, walking towards them. 'That old gas stove we used in the desert. It's still full of gas.'

'I'm not sure this is a good idea,' says Rico.

'We've got to go. You heard what Jethro said.'

'But we're not stuck in a desert this time. We can go by train, use the pickup.'

'What about Wanita?'

'We're going to be really conspicuous riding a camel, Mary.'

'I'm not leaving her.'

'Jenny can sort her, and we'll come—'

'She coming with us. She needs to be at our side. You know that.'

76

'And how's she going to cope? She's barely left the paddock for five years.'

'She'll be fine. And cross-country will be better. More places to hide until this ally shows up.' She holds her glare for a few seconds, the same look she gave the butcher all those years ago, and then pushes the stove into a saddle pocket and throws a rope round Wanita's neck, making a clicking noise with her mouth and patting the camel's side.

Rico shakes his head, knowing the conversation is over, and the decision has been made. He starts to load the blankets but freezes when a breeze blows across his body.

Mary stops patting Wanita. 'Did you feel that?'

And then it goes dark, thick, heavy clouds smothering the sky.

'They're here,' says Rico, pointing at the shadows looking down from the hillside. 'The Jinga.'

'Two of them,' she says. 'I thought there'd be more.'

'It's enough. What do we do?'

She pulls on the rope round Wanita's neck. 'The barn. We need help.'

The wind whips up into a frenzy as they drop their heads and stumble across the paddock, tugging the camel, Wanita grunting at every plod. Drizzle drops and then quickly morphs into hailstones bigger than grapes, pellets of ice pounding the top of their heads. 'Keep going,' shouts Mary, her feet slipping on the wet grass, a gale now huffing into their faces, making them gasp for breath. 'We're nearly there.'

Rico stops and looks behind him.

The Jinga haven't moved.

'Come on,' she says, reaching the barn door and yanking it open.

She pulls Wanita inside and grabs Rico's arm.

The wind and hail stop, like someone has thrown off a power switch.

'What were you doing?' she screams, pushing him into the barn and slamming the door behind them.

'Why aren't they moving? They're just standing there, and, well, the air in front of them…'

'What?'

'It looks odd, hazy, like—'

'Like the shield we saw in the desert. The one that stopped them last time.'

'It'll hold for a while.'

They look up into the eaves.

Jethro hovers over their heads and smiles at them. 'The princess has bought you some time, but the emperor can easily lift the barrier. You must go. Your ally is on the way.' He claps his smoke hands, making no sound, and the back wall of the barn falls to reveal a desert stretching to the horizon.

'But that's—'

'The hunting ground,' says Jethro, cutting across

Mary's words. 'The princess can decide the setting and she thought, with the camel—'

'This really is just a game to you, isn't it?' says Rico.

'I'm nothing more than a messenger.'

'How long do we have?'

'The emperor has twenty-four hours to track you, but the clock only starts when he manages to lift the shield and the Jinga begin their chase.'

'And this ally—'

'He'll find you.'

And with that, Jethro puffs out of existence again.

'Better get started,' says Mary, pulling her wet hair into a ponytail and tightly wrapping a band round it to hold it in place. She grabs the rope round Wanita's neck, and they walk.

Rico looks back nervously at the barn door before following them.

Two humans, keffiyehs over their faces, pulling a laden camel across a desert. What can possibly go wrong?

XXVI

Livia sighs as the vision of Rico and Mary fades into the depths of the plasma pool. She's pleased Octavius's memory stick gift has been ignored but is already wearied of a game she doesn't want to play. She wishes her father would just trust her and let her rule in her own way, but she knows he's always going to interfere. She speculates if he'd do the same with a boy or if her mother was still here. *Pointless,* she thinks, clicking her fingers towards the ceiling of the top-of-the-world atrium. *We must deal with what's real.*

A portal opens across two of the glass panels and a clock face with red digits fills the void. The digits are set at 24:00.

'The emperor has released the Jinga,' says Sebastian.

'Inevitable,' she says, clicking her fingers again.

The clock begins its countdown.

23:59; 23:58…

'I assume the gangster is waiting.'

'He's at the oasis, Your Highness, and your champion heads towards him.'

'They must be successful in their quest or the gangster delay Octavius long enough to run down the clock. Either way, we win.'

Sebastian bows his head. 'I've informed the smoke human. He'll make sure the instructions are given correctly.'

'It's essential the Jinga believe they're pursuing all of their prey.'

'Perhaps the ring will work again. Is it right to take it from them?'

'We've no choice. They'll fail without the diversion.' She waves her hand over the plasma pool. The vision of Rico, Mary and Wanita hoofing across the desert rises once more to the surface. 'We can see the woman if she's on her own now?'

Sebastian nods. 'Your father has lifted his barrier.'

'Then there's nothing more we can do.' She looks at Sini and Paloma, who stop weaving. 'Spin me a nice story.'

The teller sisters bow and resume their work.

XXVII

Rico perches back seat on the camel, having learnt from experience that Wanita gives her best game when Mary hugs her neck and tongue-clicks directly in her ear. He also wants to hide his creeping nausea, brought on by the shimmering horizon and the ship-roll of the ride. He squeezes Mary close. 'You okay?' he whispers.

She smiles at him. 'I know where we are.'

'You can't. This place is made up.'

'Don't you recognise it?'

He looks around. All he sees is sand yawning to eternity. 'A desert. They all look the same.'

'Look up,' says Mary.

He does as he's told, and the sun in front of him stings his eyes, causing him to blink furiously.

'And behind you.'

He turns his head.

Nothing. Wait. He looks forward again. 'Two suns.'

'And tonight, there'll be seven moons. We're back home.'

'I suppose the princess might as well choose somewhere familiar for us to be hunted. All we need now is to find this ally.'

'I know the answer to that as well,' she says, pointing towards the horizon. 'Mango Valley. The only oasis for miles.'

She clicks her tongue, and Rico holds on tight as the camel increases her pace.

XXVIII

Fats slumps on the sand, leans back against a mango tree trunk and looks up at the green fruit hanging over his head. His brain starts to work out how much damage a mango could do if it gave way to gravity and hit his skull. A lot, he guesses, but he's grateful for the shade of the canopy, having stripped down as far he can whilst still retaining his dignity. His clothes lie in a pile at his side – donkey jacket, woollen jumper, shirt, hat, scarf, Doc Martens, socks. He resists the urge to take off his trousers and sit there in his Y-fronts and vest, but what he'd really like to do is dive butt naked into the lake in front of him. What a place. Surrounded by sand, sitting in an oven. At least the travelling is easy. All he has to do is close his eyes and the scene shifts to wherever the princess sends him. Like the Star Trek Holodeck dropping him into a space western. Not that there's much cowboy action going on here. The only noise he's heard since the albino transported him is the rattle of a snake. He's not surprised. Who the fuck would want to live in a place like this? Not for the first time in his life he wishes his hair was shorter, but that's all part of his image. He decides to shave his head if he gets a new life, make a fresh beginning statement. He longs for town, wind and dirty rain.

He wipes his hand across his brow and takes a slug of water from the silver flask the princess gave him. Four times he's filled it already. Thank God there's loads of trees to piss behind. Sweat beads pop on his forehead, slide down his face and plop off his chin. He stands and stretches towards one of the two suns. Perspiration seeps all over his body, in places he didn't think possible. He steps back further into the shade. Sand shimmers in front of him. The trees are about ten deep circling the water, but natural archways through the branches give him a view of the wider world, allow him to keep an eye on the grainy ocean of desert in the general direction the albino told him to watch.

A noise.

A grunt.

Fats squints.

A camel carrying a man and a woman rippling towards him.

He looks at his clothes. 'Fuck that. They'll have to take me as I am.'

XXIX

Mary jumps off Wanita's back and lands on the sand. Reaching into one of the saddle pockets, she pulls out a towel and wipes her face. 'Let's get Wanita to the water.'

Rico looks at the mango trees.

'Get off her back, lazy arse,' says Mary, pulling on his boot. 'She's carried you for long enough.'

He drops wearily, takes the towel and mops his neck. 'Do you think he's here yet?'

'Jethro said he would be.'

'I can't believe we're doing this again. I thought we'd found some peace.'

'Don't look at me,' she says, grabbing Wanita's reins. 'I'm not the one being chased by a god.' She pulls the camel towards the trees. 'Anyway, what else would you be doing today?'

He catches up with her. 'We need to be wary of this guy.'

'Why do you say that? You've not met him yet.'

'I've been in his place, though. I know how desperate it can be. He's fighting for his life, like me.'

She stops walking and shoots him a look. 'Because of your sins?'

'All I'm saying is, be careful. We don't know anything about him. They'll have offered him a deal.'

'You could just tell me, you know.'

'You know everything about me. We've been together for fifteen years.'

'Which means you should trust me.'

'Hello.'

They turn towards the voice.

'There you are,' says Mary, pulling Wanita forward. 'A man in a vest, waving at us from an oasis of mango trees. What could be more normal than that?'

XXX

Fats watches the couple drag the camel to the water's edge. A brief hello, an exchange of names. The woman seems nice, but the bloke is steaming about something. And there's tension between them. He's been in those situations enough times to know prickly couple heat. Mary seems in charge, but the princess said Rico is her champion. He looks again at his clothes, thinks about putting on his shirt but feels sweat slide down his back and changes his mind.

They turn and walk back up the hill towards him.

'So,' says Mary, 'Jethro says you can help us.'

'Not sure if it'll be helpful, but there's a message from the princess.'

'Fire away,' she says, sitting down on the sand.

Rico plonks next to her, not saying a word.

'You're the champion?' says Fats.

'Is that part of the message?'

'No—'

'Then I can't see it's relevant.'

'You seem upset.'

'Shouldn't you be getting on with your job?'

'At the moment I'm wondering whether to punch you in the face. Don't take it out on me if your girlfriend's pissed with you.'

Rico jumps to his feet.

Fats does the same.

'This is going well.'

Jethro shivers in from the lake, over Wanita's head and hovers between the two men.

'Who the fuck are you?' says Fats. 'No, cancel that. What the fuck are you?'

'Have you done as you were told yet?' says Jethro.

'He's too busy sticking his nose in,' says Rico.

'Sit down, Rico,' says Mary.

Fats grins at him. 'Best do as you're told, buddy.'

'And maybe I should inform the princess how well you're handling things,' says Jethro.

Fats drops his head.

Rico laughs and sits back on the sand. 'Careful, pal. You've only just started.'

XXXI

'This doesn't make sense,' says Mary, staring at the map. 'Most of these locations can't be found in a desert.'

Fats shrugs. 'That's what they gave me. They said you'll be shifted. Once you find a crystal, the scene will change. They're good at that.'

'And these crystals will help?'

'All I know is you need them to escape, now the ring has stopped working.'

'Where do you fit in?'

'I'm bait.'

'You mean—'

'That's right. The guys chasing you, will be chasing me. And that means I need the tracker.'

'The ring?'

'Got it in one.'

'No way,' says Rico. 'This ring is our passport out of here.'

Fats picks up his shirt and starts fastening the buttons. 'No skin off my nose, but the only thing it's

90

doing at the moment is telling the guys who want to snuff you out where you are.'

Mary touches Rico's arm. 'He's right. It might be our only chance.'

'Without the ring we're stuck. We could be signing our death warrant.'

'I know, but what choice do we have?'

He hesitates, removes the ring and hands it to Fats.

Fats pushes it onto the third finger of his left hand and grins. 'Perfect fit. I knew it would be.'

'You know they'll catch you,' says Rico.

'Maybe. But, like you, I don't have many options.' He looks at Jethro. 'I need a lift to town. I stand more chance on home ground.'

'Close your eyes,' says Jethro. 'And good luck.'

XXXII

A log splinters in the blue flame of the fire, causing embers to spit and spark through the mouth of the cave and into the darkness of the valley. The smoke humans bob and weave their dance, trying to hold a stillness. 'How long has he been here?' asks Jethro, nodding towards the fur ball sitting on a rock in the corner.

'My master has agreed—'

'I'm not talking to you,' says Jethro, keeping a hard look on his brothers.

Michael rubs a misty hand over his bald head, causing wisps of smoke to break formation around him. 'Our bastard brother insisted.'

'Bernard might be able to help us,' says Thomas, pseudo-pulling at his goatee beard.

'I doubt it,' says Michael. 'That slimeball is only ever interested in himself. He wants to know what's going on with the princess's champion. He knows you've been recruited.'

'And in return?'

'Nothing specific. You know what he's like.'

Jethro faces Growler. 'You wanted to say something.'

'My master is willing to put in a good word to help your cause. He's always regretted what happened to his family—'

'Family?' spits Jethro.

'Exactly what I said,' growls Michael at the cave floor.

'My master can be a good friend, or—'

'Or what? What's stopping me telling the princess about your master?'

'You know why,' says Michael. 'She remembers nothing about us and regards him as kin. Who do you think she'll believe?'

Growler hops closer to the fire. 'My master asks you to keep him informed. Nothing more.'

'I can't see what harm it would do,' says Alfie.

Jethro looks at Michael, who shrugs.

XXXIII

Octavius runs his fingers along the bars of a bell-shaped cage hanging behind his throne. Penelope, his grey-blue harpy, with a parrot face and human legs, curls her toes tighter to the perch and then hops up and down, nibbling furiously at the feathers on her right wing. 'Calm down,' whispers Octavius. 'You're safe.'

Penelope cocks her head and looks inquisitive. 'You know what ails me,' she says, her wide eyes moist with emotion.

A cough sounds from behind Octavius. 'Captain,' he says, facing the Jinga, 'Penelope is agitated. Make sure Cicero checks her over.'

The captain glances at the harpy. 'At once, Your Majesty.'

'She's been my companion for a long time. I don't want to lose her.'

The harpy screeches.

'She seems in fine voice,' says the captain.

'There's something wrong. She pulls at her feathers. What news of the humans?'

'The Jinga are free and in pursuit.'

'Of course. Livia's party trick couldn't hold them for long. Has the clock started?'

The captain walks over to the console and studies the screen in front of him. 'We're no more than a few seconds into the time.'

'And we have the location of the humans?'

'The ring is being tracked, Your Majesty, and the Jinga have their images stored.'

'As it should be. Go and alert Cicero. And make sure the Jinga complete their mission swiftly.'

He sits on his throne and sighs as the Jinga captain marches away. He rests his hands on his stomach. This game. Battling over two humans he cares little about. And Livia, who goes beyond her remit, tries to make changes. She's smart, for a half human, but, he reasons, her mother was equally bright. Helena. His heart aches to hold her again. If only...

He looks towards the plasma pool, makes up his mind, walks over and casts his hand over the surface. Images bubble through: a waiting boatman resting on a molten lake; a swoosh through the bowels of Earth to meet a screaming inferno; and then, a charred face looms, a single horn in the middle of a forehead, like a unicorn. A laugh. Belly deep. 'Brother,' booms Wrath. 'What brings you to my humble abode?'

'There's only one reason to make contact.'

'How are your card skills?'

'I want her back.'

'Impossible.'

'Don't push me—'

'Or what? You'll break the universal agreement. The one keeping peace between gods; a pact in place since the formation of sky, the sharing of seas, land, heavens. I don't think so. You'll not risk that for a human. You stay in your domain, and we'll stay in ours.'

'You've had her long enough.'

'You shouldn't have gambled if she's so precious.'

'There's no way you won fairly. My deck, my shuffler, my dealer—'

'But no skill, Brother.'

The image fades and Octavius bites his lip. If only he could reverse time, crush his arrogance, make the decision again, but it seemed a safe bet. He had control, everything covered. And then… the humans. The brothers. They betrayed his trust. That's how it fell apart according to the bastard. Octavius wanted so much to destroy them, but the pleas of Helena while falling to the underworld made him weak.

He pushes the thoughts away.

There's nothing to be done, he tells himself.

Except, the smoke humans help Livia, and the bastard brother still plots and schemes. A human on the ecclesia along with gods. That's how weak he's been, given him influence, power. All to appease his daughter and give her some human comfort after her mother was taken. 'Maybe it's time to kill them,' he says.

XXXIV

In the shadows of the doorway, the captain watches his emperor stare silently through the window at a red dust planet sliding across the sky. A thought nags away in his mind. It's been there for a while, growing like a cancer, eating him from the inside. He's tried pushing it away, admonished himself for even letting the possibility bubble into existence, but it's stayed rooted, refused to budge. A Jinga warrior should never...

'He's troubled, sir,' says a voice behind him.

The captain closes the door to the starship's control deck. 'We need to watch him, Lieutenant. He speaks with Wrath.'

'The grief was always a worry,' says the lieutenant. 'Should we talk to the princess?'

'Too early,' says the captain, shaking his head. 'It's not clear where the ecclesia lies.'

'I'm sure the warriors will support you.'

'Thank you, Hector. We'll do what's best for the

empire. Fetch Cicero. The emperor frets about his harpy.'

Hector salutes and marches away, a puzzled look etched across his face.

The captain looks back towards the closed door. Never has a Jinga stepped in to usurp a god, but there's no precedent for what happened to the empress. He wishes the emperor would return home and take back control. Why not select a god-wife and restore pure blood? It made so much more sense when soulmates were sacrificed.

He curses under his breath.

Everything changed when a god fell in love with a human.

XXXV

Fats crunches across the gravel car park of the gala swimming baths, runs up the steps of the main entrance and heads for the boarded front doors. He remembers the baths opening, the town mayor cutting a blue ribbon, welcoming families to a state-of-the-art service. And then, two years later, the money ran out and the council couldn't afford to heat the water. He'd read in a local paper it cost seven million pounds to build. Seven mil to home smackheads, junkies and shagging teenagers, until psycho Jean had her cronies sweep away the needles and used johnnies and claim it as her execution centre.

He walks alongside a gravel-board wall, reaches one of the windows and prises away a metal grill. The smell of damp hits his nostrils, and he takes a deep breath before shoving a loaded Sainsbury's bag for life through – provisions for a couple of days – and pulling himself over the ledge and into the building. *Perfect,* he thinks, landing on the reception carpet.

The princess said he needed to hole up for twenty-four hours and, with his recent murder and Ricky No Toes' demise, he guesses Jean will keep away from here for at least a few days. He touches the ring. He really wants to bury it somewhere or dump it on an unsuspecting no-mark, throwing the god dogs off his scent, but the albino had been strict. 'Keep it with you. Get rid of it and we'll know.' Fats spits on the floor. *Fucking games*, he thinks. Same old story with God botherers, conning devotion and worship with their made-up bullshit. He pulls the grill back in place, picks up the bag and strides upstairs towards the empty pool.

He hopes the electric is on.

He's gasping for a cup of tea.

Failing that, the bottle of Johnnie Walker in his shop will have to do.

XXXVI

Mary looks at the lake and thinks about the memory stick in her dress pocket. She knows Jethro is right, but she's still curious about the man who's shared her life for the past fifteen years. The emperor's seed of doubt grows, but the ache she feels when Rico holds her, the way she melts when he looks at her, refuses to go away. She wishes he'd just tell her, trust her, put faith in their love, but only he can make that decision. She unties the saddlebags from Wanita's back and drops them onto the sand.

The camel snorts her approval, lowers her head and carries on drinking water from the lake.

'Shouldn't we keep her loaded?' says Rico. 'We only have twenty-four hours to find three crystals. The Jinga might track Fats early and head for us.'

'She needs a ten-minute break. Like you said, she's not been out of the paddock for five years. What did you think of our friend? Can he be trusted?'

'I'm not sure. But the princess knows what she's doing.'

'I feel sorry for him. They're bound to catch him, and then—'

'They might not. At least this way he has a chance.'

She looks at him thoughtfully, not wanting to push the question, but curiosity overwhelms her. 'Is that the choice they offered you?'

'I'm guessing our stories are similar. We're disposable, pawns in a game.'

'That's horrible.'

'We're lucky,' says Rico, unbuttoning his shirt.

'What are you doing?'

'I need to cool down.'

'And we need to find that crystal. It's here somewhere, according to the map.'

'If the camel can have a ten-minute break, so can we.' He drops his shirt to the sand, pulls off his jeans and pants, and races into the water. 'You coming in? It's lovely.'

'I can't believe you. We're being chased by afterlife warriors.'

'And we still will be in ten minutes. Come in.'

She hesitates for a second, unbuttons her cotton dress, throws it next to the saddlebags and strips off her underwear. She races into the water and dives under the surface.

Rico swims over and holds her. 'You okay?'

'Strangely, yes. It feels like we're doing something now.'

'They were always going to come. We knew that.'

'I'd got used to the peace, I guess.'

He kisses her.

She pulls his body closer. 'Ten minutes?' she says, wrapping her legs around him.

Wanita grunts at them from the shore.

XXXVII

Fats curses as the door slams behind him, an echo reverberating round the high-ceilinged auditorium that is home to the empty pool. He stays still for a second. Nothing. The place is empty. He surveys the spectator seats rising in rows and finds the spot where Jean and her posse sat to watch the Rottweilers rip him to shreds. He can't complain. He's been in the punter seat next to Jean many times, laughing and cheering the screams. That's the life he landed and the game he followed. Sitting in silence or protesting meant feeding Jean's paranoia. Not a good place to be. Ignore Jean's rules and you stopped breathing. That's how it worked.

He takes in the empty pool.

Spotless, but he knew it would be – a ritual clean-up followed religiously by the posse. High-pressure hose, scrubbing brushes; a mincer for the body parts the dogs refused to eat. Immaculate. He'd challenge the *Silent Witness* guys to find any forensic here. Jean joked that she could sell the instruction manual and make a fortune. A perfect assassination. Fats grins. To be fair, she's never been caught, and the body count must be well into double figures.

He hauls the shopping bag onto his back and walks down the metal steps, wishing the pool was full of chlorinated water. Swimming relaxes him or, to be more precise, floating, lying on his back, staring at the ceiling. He could do with that now. A gentle drift into oblivion.

He lands on the concrete base and sits in the corner. The sadness of a swimming pool denied water washes over him. He tries to swallow the emotion but out it gurgles.

He reaches into the shopping bag, grabs the whisky bottle, unscrews the cap and takes a slug. 'Stupid bastard,' he tells himself, taking another slug.

XXXVIII

Bernard looks again at the rolled-out parchment in his hands. 'A summons,' he says, shaking his head. 'From Octavius. Is this genuine?'

'It bears the royal seal,' says Growler, 'and was delivered by Jinga warriors.'

'Octavius doesn't summon people. He might have them arrested or killed but not called for an audience. Does the princess know?'

'I don't know, Master.'

'*His Majesty would be grateful if I could join him…* That doesn't even sound like Octavius.'

'Perhaps he wants your advice on the game. It could be an opportunity.'

'I should discuss this with the princess.'

'The Jinga are waiting for you.'

'I don't like being bounced. What's going on with the humans?'

'Jethro returns today. He's agreed to update us later.'

'And meantime, I have to waste my time on this summons.'

'I don't see any other option, Master.'

Bernard walks over to the attic window. 'We'll go to the smoke humans on our way. Something doesn't smell right. Find me that infernal cassock they like me to wear. And tell the Jinga I'll be with them shortly.'

XXXIX

Mary and Rico sit side by side and study the map they've unrolled on the sand and weighted down with two rocks. 'Three locations,' says Mary. 'Only one of them a desert.'

'It looks like it's in that direction, away from Mango Valley,' says Rico, pointing into the sun, 'but it doesn't say what or where we find it.'

'We know it's a crystal.'

'But it must be somewhere. It can't just be lying on the sand. And what's it for?'

She jumps to her feet. 'Let's get going. It'll be obvious when we see it.'

'We could just stay here.'

'And wait for the Jinga?'

'Without the ring, they can't trace us.'

'And what happens when they catch Fats? They're bound to come for us.' She pulls him to his feet. 'We need to do what the princess says. You sound like you're losing faith.'

He brushes sand off his jeans. 'I just wish we could be normal, live a proper life.'

'You're a champion of an afterlife princess, hanging round with a crazy woman and a camel. How can that ever be normal?'

'True,' he says, pulling her close and kissing her.

'I'm still curious about your past life.'

'I'll tell you. I promise. But let's get to a safe place first.'

He picks up his shirt and walks towards Wanita.

Mary pats her dress pocket to check the memory stick is safe and follows him.

*

Wanita pricks her ears and chews contentedly on her bottom lip as Mary's tongue clicks encourage a rolling pace across the desert. They plod towards the sun, Mary scratching the camel's rough neck fur, making Wanita fart, snort and speed up.

'I swear that camel understands your every word,' whispers Rico, nuzzling into Mary's back.

'Of course she does. How are you feeling?'

'Like throwing up. I understand now why they call them ships. It's like being tossed about in the surf.'

'You're such a drama queen.'

He swallows hard, trying to keep bile from rising in his throat, his nausea surging with Wanita's rolling gait. Mary's questions circle his head, weighing him down like steel toe-capped boots. Sins from another life. They're always there in his mind. A car; a red-headed boy; the smell of Bacardi. He stares at the sand, trying to focus on one point. 'You'll have to stop,' he says, jumping down and landing with a thud. He retches once, and then again.

Mary drops beside him and puts her hand on his back. 'You seemed okay earlier.'

He wipes spittle from his lips. 'The travel pills have worn off.'

'Travel pills,' she says, laughing. 'To ride a camel.'

'It treats the vertigo,' he says, spitting into the sand. 'They're in the saddlebag. I'd better take some more.'

She reaches into the pocket he's staring at and pulls out a box of tablets, popping two from the foil and handing them to him.

He grabs a waterbag, throws the pills in his mouth and takes a slug. They stand side by side looking at the dunes, the sun beating down on them. He takes another drink.

'Better?' says Mary.

'It will be.'

She pulls the map from her pocket and studies it.

'Are we still on track?'

'Hard to tell. Your princess will make it obvious. We just have to trust her.'

*

An hour later, Rico wobbles on Wanita's back, grateful for the sickness pills settling his nausea. Even so, he'll be happier when this ride is over. The thought of night-time bothers him. Ten years they'd lived in a desert on the two suns and seven moons world, and he'd never got used to the thirty-degree temperature drop at night. Still, the blankets will help, and it's a good excuse to cuddle Mary close and share body heat. That possibility pleases him, and he hopes they don't find the crystal before the sun goes down. He sucks on a roll-up and blows smoke towards the sky, knowing they're bad for him, but he reasons his fitness regime more than compensates. Quid pro quo. Something his old schoolteacher used to say in a previous existence, but he tries not to dwell on her.

'I hope you're not blowing that in my hair,' says Mary.

'Nowhere near,' he says, throwing the butt to the floor.

'Those things will kill you.'

'Unless a Jinga warrior gets me first.'

She kisses him. 'How's the sickness, Champ?'

'Not bad. How far do you think? We've been going a couple of hours now. It seems closer on the map.'

She takes a swig of water. 'I'm not sure the map is helpful. Just a general direction pointer.'

'I might be imagining this,' says Rico, 'but there's something up ahead.'

She shades her eyes and squints. 'I can't see anything.'

'There, on top of that dune. Maybe not. It looks like… there it is again. A light.'

'It's the sun reflecting off… no… you're right. But that could be anything.'

'It's all we've got,' says Rico.

She pulls the keffiyeh over her mouth, clicks her tongue and pats Wanita's neck.

*

They reach the edge of the dune and slide off the camel's back.

'That's impossible,' says Rico.

In front of them, hovering in mid-air, is a round, buttercup-yellow door, edged with white light, looking like a framed sun. A gold knocker, shaped like a lion's head, sits in its centre, red rubies for eyes and a string of diamonds glistening in its mouth.

Mary starts to walk up the dune.

'What are you doing?'

'I'm going to knock on the door,' she says, facing him.

'Do you think we should?'

'Rico, do you see anything else here that's weird

enough to have been sent by a princess from the afterlife?' She carries on walking.

He races up the sand and grabs her arm. 'Let me.'

'Why?'

'Because I'm the champion.'

'And I'm a girl.'

'I didn't mean that. It might not be expecting you. I feel worried enough that we haven't got the ring as a passport. At least let's give it something it might recognise.'

She looks at the sand for a second. 'Fair enough.'

He hesitates.

'Go on, Champ. It's not going to come to you.'

He trudges up the dune, expecting warmth from the light as he gets closer, but a cool breeze tickles his face, bringing much needed relief from the blistering sun. He hears Mary walking behind him and knows she's struggling to stop herself overtaking and beating him to the knocker. There's part of him that wants to let her, but he's sure his rationale is right.

He reaches the door.

'It's beautiful,' says Mary into his neck. 'Look at the scroll on the face.'

'I guess it's what you'd expect from a god,' he says.

He lifts the lion's head and then gently replaces it. 'How hard should I knock?'

'Just knock, Rico.'

He lifts the knocker again and bangs three times.

*

They step back as the door, rather than swing open, divides itself diagonally across its centre, each half swooshing away, leaving a round portal of white light beaming at them. They hear scuffling, like something being dragged, and then, a figure hobbles towards them: a man wearing a leather, knee-length tunic, breeches tied at the waist and ankles, a red cloak flung round his shoulders; a pair of worn caligae covering his feet, the stitching coming loose along the seams. He carries a sword and shield, and his long, waist-length, grey hair flows freely down his back. Reaching the edge of the sand, he bends over for a second to catch his breath.

Mary rushes forwards.

'No further,' he gasps, standing up straight and holding out his sword, making her skid to a halt. 'Tell me who you are. Why have you summoned me?'

'The princess sent us. We've come for the crystal.'

He drops to his knees and bursts into tears.

She wraps her arms round his shoulders and tries to comfort him, but he sobs uncontrollably into his tunic. She can see his grey, aged skin, flapping off his bones like washing on a line. Three gold leopards surround a dragon in the centre of his shield, but the gold has flaked in places, and tinges of rust stain the sword blade.

'Who are you?' says Rico.

The man sniffs and wipes his eyes. Mary removes her keffiyeh, hands it to him and he blows his nose. 'My name is of no consequence,' he says, 'but the princess allows me to guard the crystal and now my job is done.'

'How long have you been here?' she says, rubbing the man's back, feeling knobbles of backbone through his leather tunic.

'Millennia,' he says, shrugging his shoulders.

'On your own?' says Rico, looking into the portal.

'There's been no need for anyone else,' says the man, putting his hands on the sand and trying to push himself upwards. He stumbles and Mary places a hand under his arm and helps him to his feet. 'Thank you,' he says, steadying himself before turning back to the light and ambling along the tunnel. 'Follow me. Your crystal is inside.'

*

They copy the man's snail pace and keep two steps behind. It's like marking time along a torch beam, but one that completely encircles them from the outside world. The intensity of light draws tears from their eyes, and they blink to keep focus. Not that there's much to see, except for white glare stretching into the distance. 'We should be wearing sunglasses,' says Rico.

The man gives him a puzzled look.

'To protect our eyes.'

'You get used to it. It's not far.'

'Look,' says Mary, pinching Rico's arm.

Ahead of them, at the end of the tunnel, awaits an alcove. They carry on walking and, finally, with a weary sigh, the man slumps into a wing chair, reaches out and rests his hand on a round, football-sized, labradorite crystal sitting in the centre of an oak table. 'This is yours. Take it.'

Mary leans closer to the crystal. Sparkles from the corridor light reflect at her. 'It's beautiful.'

'It misses the sun,' says the man.

'Is this your home?' says Rico, looking round the alcove.

The space they're in is no bigger than a cell, with just the armchair and table, and bare walls and ceiling pulsing with white light. There's no evidence of anyone existing here for a day, let alone a millennium.

'It's where the princess asked me to stay until I'd done my duty,' says the man, closing his eyes briefly before opening them again and pushing himself to his feet. 'And now you must go.'

'What will happen to you?' says Mary, squeezing his hand.

He squeezes back and smiles. 'You're a kind soul. I'm glad it's you. The princess will decide my fate. Now go.'

Rico picks up the crystal from the table. 'Thank you for looking after it.'

'Yes,' says Mary, kissing the man on the cheek.

He touches his face, slumps on his chair and watches them walk back along the light corridor. From the corner of the alcove, a shadow emerges. 'They've gone,' says the man. 'My task is complete.'

'You've done well. You'll be rewarded.'

'And you, my companion in life, you'll take me to my death.'

The shadow casts its hand across the man's arm.

'That's all I ask,' says the man.

*

The portal door bangs into place as they step back onto the sand.

Wanita watches them slide down the dune, Rico holding the amber crystal to his chest like a goalie clutching a football.

'You been keeping guard?' says Mary, scratching the camel's head.

A lip curl from Wanita reveals her protruding, stained teeth.

'We got it,' says Rico, setting the crystal down and kneeling next to it.

'The man's right,' says Mary, crouching beside him and looking into the labradorite. 'The sun makes its surface translucent, and the veins of mineral look like they're alive.'

'One down, two to go. Where's the map?'

'In the saddlebag,' she says, standing up and retrieving the parchment.

They roll it out on the sand, sitting the crystal on one of its corners.

'Do you think the man will be alright?' says Mary.

'The princess will take care of him. He's done what she asked.'

'Maybe we should have brought him with us.'

'It's none of our business. We must look after ourselves.'

'It all seems—'

'Let's concentrate on finding the next crystal,' he says, tracing his finger round the spot on the map marked X2. 'This doesn't look right.'

'Like I said, the other locations aren't in a desert.'

'You've done well so far.'

They turn towards Wanita.

Jethro hovers over the camel, grinning at them.

'If I remember rightly,' says Mary, 'you shifted Fats when he closed his eyes.'

'And that's exactly what I'll do for you.'

XL

Fats takes another slug of whisky and looks at the bottle. A quarter empty, but it's not doing it for him. Normally, he can rely on Mr Walker to dull pain, but this time the sadness is sticking, gripping him like a never-ending bellyache. He scans the empty pool. The memories should disturb him, but, for the most part, he had a job to do, and he did it well. In the end, he became the hunted, but that's karma. Eventually the world catches up and bites back.

He rolls his finger across the ring. White gold, bridge and spot diamonds. Classy. Not a surprise. A gift from a princess to her champion. *Champion of what?* Mary looked like she had more about her. Rico must have been useful. Same as it ever was. Everyone on the make, twisting to get their bidding done. Like him, now. Another shot at life, but it's a suicide mission. Maggot bait. Dispensable. The albino's expression when he looked at him said it all.

But he's still here. Rolling with the punches.

He screws the cap back on the bottle and pushes it into the shopping bag.

A noise from the landing.

He jumps to his feet and looks at the gallery. Surely, they haven't found him already. The princess said they'd chase him, track him through the ring, but he'd expected more time to get his head together.

The noise again.

He climbs the steps out of the pool, heads towards the landing, but ducks behind a row of seats when a door opens and then slams shut. He hears footsteps, high heels click-clacking, in-between the back two rows. They stop. One of the chairs creaks. A woman with a radio tuned to Steve Wright. Queen's 'I Want to Break Free' echoes off the pool roof. Of all the scenarios he imagined of his afterlife pursuers, this wasn't anywhere on the chart. He crawls along to the aisle, lifts his head. A plume of cigarette smoke rises to the ceiling. He recognises the smell. It can't be.

Spiky blonde hair, puffing on a More menthol; stilettoes tapping out a rhythm to Freddie's vocals. A surge of adrenalin races through his body. *Calm down*, he tells himself, but panic consumes him. This woman had him chewed by Rottweilers. A psychopath and she's on his trail. But that can't be right. There's no way Jean is his pursuer, and she's not behaving like she knows he's there.

The chair creaks again as she stands; the radio

goes silent, and the heels click-clack back towards the aisle and down the stairs towards the empty pool.

Fats scrambles underneath the seats, watching through the legs of a chair as she passes his hiding row. She reaches the bottom of the steps and sits with her legs hanging over the poolside. Another suck of More menthol, an exhale of smoke. She puts the radio at her side. What the fuck is she doing? She looks sober, but she's acting pissed.

A cramp starts in his left leg, so he shifts it, scratching the floor with his Doc Marten.

Jean looks round.

He holds his breath.

She turns her body, pushes her fingers into the grid of a drain next to her and wrenches the cover free. She reaches inside and lifts out a brown paper bag.

Fats grins.

Jean never did trust banks.

XLI

Cicero, a wizened man with wisps of grey hair clinging to his head, releases the catch on the harpy's cage door and lets it fall open. He pushes his arm inside and offers it to Penelope. She jumps onto his wrist and sits perfectly still as he pulls her slowly into the room. 'What's the matter?' he whispers, lifting his thin-framed spectacles and dropping them to his nose tip. He double-checks the wiry arms are secure round his ears before peering into the harpy's face and stroking the top of her head with one finger. He makes a shushing noise. 'Has something upset you?'

Penelope blinks at him. 'It's time to bring her back.'

Octavius watches from his throne, mesmerised. So much love for a fellow creature. 'I don't want her to suffer, but sending her back to an egg means waiting for maturity before she becomes a good companion. I need her now.'

'She's had many reincarnations,' says Cicero,

stroking Penelope's head again, 'but she's not in pain. Just grieving.' He kisses the harpy lightly on the beak, pushes his hand back in the cage and waits for Penelope to jump on her perch. 'I'll mix a seed bag. Give her an energy boost.'

'I envy you, Cicero.'

'Majesty?'

'Your connection to these creatures. You're suited to the work.'

Cicero smiles, closes the cage door and drops the catch. 'It's a privilege to serve you in such a way.'

He bows and leaves the room.

Octavius stands and walks over to the cage. He leans closer to the bars and mimics the shushing noise made by Cicero. Penelope opens her beak but this time makes no sound. 'Quite right. We'll rest in silence for a while.' He sits back on his throne, sucking in the moment of quiet, and wishes Helena could be here. Hours they'd spent in comfortable togetherness, when no words were needed. He'd pretend to read but secretly watch her as she embroidered, occasionally looking up at him with a demure and gentle smile. He winces as sadness swamps him and, not for the first time, curses his stupidity. A lump drops in the back of his throat. Cicero is right with his diagnosis of grief.

He jolts as the captain marches into the control room, comes to a halt, clicks his heels together and salutes.

'Your Majesty, there's a problem with the game.'

Octavius wants to scream, 'I don't care. Leave me in peace'. That's what he should say, but, instead, he feels the trap of his emperor's mask slam back into place. He takes a deep swallow and sits up on his throne. 'You assured me all was well.'

'We've discovered two trails for the humans.'

'The ring and the memory stick. I'd assumed you were tracking both.'

'We are, sir, but they're in completely different parts of the planet. The memory stick lies within the hunting ground, but the ring is in a populated town, something we'd not planned for.'

'The humans have separated?'

'They still run together, but the ring is with someone else.'

'Livia has found an ally, given me a false trail.'

'We could capture the champion and his woman and finish the game early.'

'No. I want the ring, and the princess needs a lesson. She's not thought of the memory stick being traced.'

'Yes, sir.'

'Send your lieutenant after the ally, but you know the sensitivities outside the hunting ground. I'm assuming the warriors are in pursuit of the other humans.'

'They're about to reach them, sir.'

'Take them by surprise.'

The captain salutes again and hurries out of the room.

XLII

Fats eases back in a spectator chair and looks at the empty pool. He rests his hand on two brown paper bags in his lap. Five grand in each. What he'd have given for that in life, but it's a waste to him now. Even so, he's emptied Jean's drain stash, leaving her with just the couple of wads she stuffed in her pocket before she left. A bit of flash cash to get her through the week. Taking these bags will hurt, but she'll have other stash holes round town. He'd love to let her know it was him, but that crazy albino and the princess will be watching. Well, they can't begrudge him a bit of revenge. They probably expect it of him.

He grabs the envelopes, breaks the seals and tips twenty-pound notes in a pile on the concrete floor, taking a moment to register what he's doing, something that would have had him certified in life, but he has to move on. He strikes a match, ignites a couple of notes and watches as the flames spread.

Ten grand up in smoke; Johnnie Walker; holing up here. All a waste. He needs to get back on the streets. Whatever's coming for him might get slowed down in a crowd. He's running down the clock. Time's the only thing on his side right now.

He touches the ring and decides not to wait for the ashes.

XLIII

A gentle tap on the door of the captain's quarters.

'Come in. It's open.'

'You wanted to see me, sir,' says Hector, entering the room.

The captain drops his bare feet off a carbon fibre pouffe and pushes himself up in his leather chair. 'Thank you for joining me. Drink?'

'Is that what I think it is?' says Hector, nodding at a tray of crystal glass vials on a drinks table.

The captain smiles, reaches over, uncorks two vials and holds one out towards his guest. 'Adrenochrome. The emperor lets me have a few bottles a year.'

Hector takes the drink, sits in a second armchair and sips the pink solution. He puts his head back to savour the hit, feeling a whoosh of relaxant reach his brain. 'I thought the princess outlawed production.'

'A small human farm on the edge of the universe. Very respectable.'

'Shame they die when it's drawn from their adrenal gland.'

'Worth it, though,' says the captain, taking a drink from his own vial and licking his lips. 'I have a mission for you. It'll mean going off base for a while.'

'What would you like me to do?'

'Visit the planet and catch a human. We've not secured him in a hunting area, which means you going native, so to speak.'

'Can I ask why?'

'All part of a game. Locate him from a tracker and bring him back here. The tracker is a ring, a gift from the princess. That needs to come back as well.'

'I'll leave at once,' says Hector, taking another sip of adrenochrome, his mind shifting down a few more gears as the sweet nectar soaks his system.

'Hallucinogenic for humans,' says the captain. 'Their perfect high, but for gods, a chillout sweetie. Don't you agree?'

'It's doing it for me,' says Hector, swirling his vial.

'Before you get too relaxed, there's something else. I'm worried about the emperor.'

Hector feels the atmosphere in the room chill. He crosses his legs, and his whole body stiffens as he looks towards the closed door. He remembers a human history book poster: *Walls Have Ears* emblazoned across the centre in scarlet-red ink. A voice in his head whispers, *Be careful.* The conversation earlier was bad enough, but here, in the captain's private quarters, it feels like plotting. 'The emperor?' he says, watching the captain lean over to the drinks tray and retrieve two more vials.

'He grieves his empress, seeks answers from the monk. You know the rumours?'

'A fixed deck. But the emperor punished the brothers.'

'Ah, the unmentionables. I think he's having second thoughts, suspects the monk of involvement, but the bastard has influence and the last thing we need is a split ecclesia.'

'Does the princess know about the others?'

'She has no idea. The emperor wiped her memory of the smoke humans, and she sees the monk as a trusted uncle. The only thing left of her mother.'

'What are you going to do?'

'Wait. I need to know you're with me.'

Hector hesitates, places his empty vial on his lap and takes a full one held out by the captain.

'I see you have doubts.'

'It's just, well… I'm not sure what I can do.'

'Be ready. Our first duty is to the ecclesia. Don't you agree?'

Hector meets his eyes. He feels cornered. Whatever road he takes risks a high-impact crash. Right now, in this room, he has no choice. 'Of course,' he says, uncorking the adrenochrome.

XLIV

The barman whizzes a shot glass full of Pernod crème de menthe along the bar. Fats catches it with a single swoop and downs it in one. 'Number four,' shouts the barman. 'Never thought I'd do that with a liqueur.'

Fats grins. 'Better get me a lager. I can feel my legs going numb.'

'Coming right up,' says the barman, pulling on the tap. He drops a paper coaster and sets the pint down. 'Do me a favour. Keep an eye on things while I nip for a Jimmy Riddle.'

'No problem, mate,' says Fats. 'I don't think I'll get caught in a rush.'

The barman laughs and disappears towards the gents.

Fats checks out the jukebox and presses the buttons for The Boomtown Rats' 'Rat Trap'. He sips his beer and takes in his fellow customers. The touchy-feely couple have disappeared, probably to find a bed, judging by the way things were heating up earlier. The old man is still there. Fats wonders what his story is, how he arrived on his own in a bar night after night. He makes a note to send him a drink over when the barman comes back. He might as well put the princess's credit card to good use.

His attention turns to the new bloke. The one who came in ten minutes ago, ordered a whisky and plonked himself in one of the alcoves. There's something about him that Fats can't straighten in his head. First, it's the way he's dressed. A brown trench coat, cords and monkey boots. Nothing wrong so far. But then he's wearing a trilby and has empty hoop ring holes at the side of each nostril. Like he's missed a couple of beats with the fashion. And he keeps sneaking sly looks, staring at something in his lap for a few seconds and then at Fats, like he's weighing up what to do next.

Fats makes up his mind and walks over. 'Do I know you, mate?'

The man lifts his head, straightens his hat and looks Fats in the eye. 'You're expecting me,' he says, nodding at the ring. 'Sit down.'

Fats doesn't move.

'You've put a lot of booze away,' says the man. 'There's no way you can run. Sit down. I don't want a scene.'

Cursing his carelessness, Fats does as he's told. 'They made you sound like some monster, not a plain Joe. What happens now?'

'We leave the bar calmly, and I take you back for judgement.'

'You mean death.'

The man shrugs. 'Not my call.'

'I'm guessing that's what you've been looking at under the table. A tracking screen. I suppose telling you to fuck off isn't an option.'

'It'll get you dead. And it makes things messy, with more paperwork. At least my way you get to plead your case.'

'Hey, buddy,' shouts the barman. 'You ready for another?'

'Ignore him,' says the man.

'That'll look odd. Let me say goodbye and settle my tab. And then we'll walk out together.'

The man looks at the bar.

The barman smiles and then waves. 'How about two shots this time? One for your friend.'

'Two minutes,' says the man. 'And I'll be watching.'

Fats stands and walks over to the bar. 'No more for me, pal. I need to be off. What's the damage?'

The barman gives him a disappointed face. 'You sure? I've got plenty more of that toothpaste drink.'

Fats slides his credit card towards him and leans closer. 'Take a good tip. And do me a favour. The guy over there's an old friend. Drop him a bottle of scotch and make a fuss. I'm just popping for a piss.'

'Sure thing, buddy,' says the barman, reaching

behind him and pulling a bottle of whisky off the shelf. He walks out from behind the bar. 'Hey, pal, this is from your old mate over there. What—'

The bar door slams.

Hector pushes the barman to the floor and chases after Fats.

XLV

The smoke humans barely acknowledge their visitors, preferring instead to enjoy a roaring cave fire and the view from their hillside retreat – an ink-blue night sky with a moon half veiled by a single cloud, giving the impression of a smile.

Bernard stands in front of them, clenching his hands to still his impatience. He's conscious of the Jinga soldier waiting for him at the atrium. 'It's to the emperor's advantage,' he'd told the man, and then, when the warrior had looked reluctant, reminded him of his status – not the first time he'd pulled the ecclesia badge to secure a deal. Even so, he knows he's on borrowed time. 'I need to know what's happening, Jethro. I've been summoned.'

Growler, picking up on his master's mood, bobs restlessly at his side.

Jethro turns towards Michael. 'Can you hear the sound of chickens coming home to roost?'

'I can,' says Michael. 'Our "brother" might be about to face his maker.'

All the smoke humans laugh, causing their images to waft and interlock, creating a hotch-potch of faces, legs, arms and torsos. They separate once more, squeezing the cloudy line of their lips together to stifle any residual sniggers.

'Enjoy your joke,' says Bernard, 'but it's not me blown about by a wisp of wind.'

Jethro looks at his brothers, the smile gone from his face, and then back at Bernard. 'The humans are being pursued by the Jinga, but there are two trails. One of them has moved from the hunting ground.'

'The gangster,' says Bernard. 'And the Jinga pursue him?'

'The lieutenant seeks him out.'

'And the champion?'

'He and the woman search for crystals. The ring has failed, but the princess sends them to the well. What will you do with this information?'

'Nothing yet, but it may prove useful.'

'And how does that benefit us?'

'I'll do what I can. The princess trusts my word.'

'And the emperor?'

'Uncertain, but that may not be a problem.'

Jethro gives him a puzzled look.

'Nothing for you to worry about, Brother. Leave the politics to me.'

Bernard exits the cave and hikes back down the hillside, Growler scuttling behind him.

'Leave it to him,' snarls Michael. 'Do you trust what he says?'

'Not one iota,' says Jethro.

XLVI

Fats races along rain-soaked pavements, dodging up and down a matrix of shitty alleyways, past overflowing rubbish bins keeping guard at the back gates of terraced houses. He puffs hard and takes gulps of breath to feed his lungs. Pernod crème de menthe soaks his veins. 'Fucking wanker,' he mutters, cursing his schoolboy error. The last thing a runner does when he's being tracked is stay in one place. He checks the ring. His racing mind considers chucking it away, over one of the walls, but that'll just replace this nutter with the sour-faced albino. Sweat beads pop all over his body as he dodges again.

Still running, he glances behind. No sight or sound of monkey boots man. He'd heard a couple of shouts along the street from the pub but no gunshot. That must be his weapon of choice. What else could he have? 'Anything, you twat. He's a warrior sent by God.' He bites his lip. This talking to himself is becoming a habit. It'll draw attention. He turns into an alley with no street lights, the bulbs stone-popped by kids desperate for something to fill their empty lives. A scenario he recognises.

He stops, leans against a wall and throws up. A bile pool smell of peppermint and aniseed hits his nostrils. He laughs. As sick goes, it's pretty pleasant. He looks at the sky. Moonlight and drizzle smack him in the face. He wipes his mouth. What now? He has to keep moving. The ring will let monkey boots keep tabs, but it's not easy to catch a moving target. Especially one who knows the streets like he laid every brick and tarmacked every road. Monkey boots doesn't want a fuss. That's a weakness, limits the choice of execution ground. All Fats has to do is keep ahead of him for twenty-four hours. He must be well into that time by now.

Traffic noise from a main road.

Keep on the move without getting knackered, and, like every junkie and waster, try to keep warm for free.

He knows exactly where to do both.

He heads into town to jump on the night bus.

XLVII

Rico freezes at the scene in front of him.

A meadow of purple and white rhododendron bushes sways in the breeze next to a millpond with two naked nymph statues in its centre, a boy and girl holding hands, a fountain gushing from each of their mouths. Water splashes into the pond, sending ripples across its surface. He gulps as the sweet scent of blossoms fills his nostrils.

Wanita grunts and Mary tickles the camel's head before unrolling the map parchment and studying it. 'It's this way,' she says, tugging Wanita along the bank of the pond.

The hairs on the back of Rico's hands twitch; goosebumps rise on his arms. He wants to run. He swallows hard and drags his dry tongue along a cigarette roll-up paper, catches a whiff of loose tobacco, crimps the strips together and shakily puts the fag in his mouth. He strikes a match, ignites the shag and takes a long draw, blowing smoke towards the meadow.

'Come on,' shouts Mary.

He takes another drag and then walks quickly up a hill along a dirt track to catch up with her. 'Sorry,' he says, coming to her side.

'We need to keep moving.'

They plod in silence, finally reaching the hill's summit.

Mary unrolls the map again and traces the route with her finger. 'It ends here.'

Rico takes in the moribund millpond and the sweep of rhododendron bushes. A fresh wave of anxiety washes through him as a screeching circle of fruit bats fly over. He watches the bats get smaller and smaller as they head towards the sun. 'I feel…'

His words trail away, and she looks at him. 'Sit down. You've gone really pale.'

He plonks himself on the dirt track.

Mary kneels and unscrews the lid on the water flask. 'Drink. You look like you're about to faint.'

He gulps greedily. 'I've been here before,' he says, still staring at the millpond. 'When I died this—'

'There's someone watching us,' she says, pointing to the other side of the summit.

A woman, hands on hips, barefoot, wearing a full-length red linen dress.

Rico throws the cigarette butt to the floor. 'I'll go,' he says, trying to push himself off the ground.

'Stay here,' says Mary. 'Take some deep breaths. I'll go.'

She stands, moves a few steps, but stops when the woman holds up her hand.

'Who are you?' the woman shouts. 'What's your business here?'

'The princess sent us. We're searching for a crystal.'

The woman clicks her fingers, disappears and then emerges right next to them. 'Come with me.'

Mary takes Rico's arm and helps him to his feet.

He stumbles and stares at the woman. 'I know you.'

The woman ignores him and walks away.

'Come on,' says Mary, looking anxiously at Rico. 'Let's do as she asks.'

*

They follow the woman in silence along the dirt track, which peters out and morphs into a sandy avenue of coconut palms and mango trees.

Mary's bare feet get dusted with each step through her open-toed sandals by talcum powder sand. She can see the end of the avenue, marked by the fallen trunks of two trees, a natural archway. A few more steps and, through the gap, a sea emerges, caressing and kissing the shore, rolling backwards and forwards; backwards and forwards. She licks her lips. A taste of salty air, the sight of sunlight sparkling off the water, the sound of lapping waves and the heady citrus aroma from the plants. Her senses ping into overload.

'It's exactly as I remember it,' says Rico.

'It's gorgeous,' says Mary, stepping through the archway. She drops Wanita's reins. An azure sea, melding with a cloudless sky, empties her thoughts and shuts her mind into silence. Nothing but crab tracks cover the white sand beach. A boat chugs along the horizon, reaches the periphery of her view, looks like it's in danger of falling off the edge of the world and then turns round, crawling back on itself. 'What is this place?'

'Limbo,' says Rico, kneeling and picking up a small piece of sun-bleached coral, which he turns over and over in his left hand. He looks at the light cyan blue of the lagoon and follows its trail beyond the reef to the inky dark of the deep. He can't think of anything else to say.

'You were rescued last time,' says the woman, suddenly right in front of them. 'The princess had another destiny for you.'

'I don't understand,' says Mary.

'He knows. This is where lost souls wait for God's judgement.'

Rico grabs Mary's hand and gives her a pleading look.

'It's okay,' she whispers, hugging him and stroking the back of his head. She studies the woman's face.

Dark brown, almost black, eyes stare out at her like they're on stalks ready to pop; a line of freckles run from cheek to cheek across the bridge of her nose, like a join-the-dots invitation. 'Do you have the crystal?'

'I can give you what you seek.'

Rico eases Mary away, throws the coral into the ocean, rubs his hands together to brush off the sand and stands up. 'This place…'

Mary reaches into her dress pocket, pulls out a paper tissue and hands it to him.

He blows his nose.

'The crystal?' says Mary.

The woman nods towards the boat. 'It's safe.'

'How do we reach it?'

'The keeper has instructions. We need to wait at the jetty.' She takes a few steps along the beach, leaving no footprints in the sand, clearly expecting them to follow.

'Wait,' says Rico. 'Why is it so empty? Before, there were thousands.'

'The beach is full,' says the woman, turning and holding out her arms. 'You don't belong here, which means you can't see or hear them, but they're watching you.'

Mary and Rico look along the shore. Nothing. Complete stillness.

'Close your eyes.'

They do as they're told.

Something drops in their heads. A mumble, louder, louder, and then, the banshee howl of a crowd cuts through their brains and rips at their eardrums. Their eyes flash open.

The woman walks away.

'Let's get out of here,' says Mary, pulling Wanita.

*

Rico trudges along the claggy sand, trying his best to keep up with them, not wanting to be left alone. He sees Mary look back and give him a sympathy smile. 'Walk higher up the beach,' she shouts, making herself heard over the waves hitting the shore, 'or take your shoes off.'

'I'm fine,' he shouts back.

He looks at Mary's feet. She's slipped her sandals and gone barefoot, which means her and Wanita are splashing through the water. Getting his boots off means undoing the laces, causing delay, and that isn't going to happen. He tells himself the walkway to the jetty sits up ahead, not far at all, and tries to control his breathing, conscious that every step brings him closer, but he's struggling to gasp in enough oxygen. Every so often, he hears a crunch underneath his feet, a reminder of empty shells and fossils, a trigger to make him remember the dead. He tries to soften his step, not wanting to wake the ghosts. The banshee scream has brought it all back. Hands reaching out in a fog of human bodies, pleading to be saved. Every faltering step he takes passes through and ignores another wailing soul. He knows the despair. Howling for gods to show mercy. The princess heard his pleas and plucked him to do her bidding, but the beach has left its scar.

And now fate has brought him back.

No delays.

He tries to speed up, but sand collapses underneath him. It's like this place knows he's a fugitive and plots to suck him back. The sun beats down. His chest tightens as he gasps for breath, and he falls to his knees. Faces loom at him over and over. 'Save me,' each of them screams. 'Save me.'

'Breathe,' says Mary, suddenly at his side. 'Deep breaths from your stomach. Like this.'

In, out. In, out.

He follows her rhythm.

In, out. In, out.

Slowly his head clears; the souls fall away; and the screams subside.

She puts a flask to his lips.

He drinks, and then again.

'Better?' she says.

He nods and takes another drink.

'The beach can do that,' says the woman, now standing next to Mary. 'The keeper is on his way. We need to move.' She walks back towards Wanita, who stares nonchalantly in their direction from the water's edge, chewing on her bottom lip.

'I see them,' says Rico. 'They're in my head.'

Mary unties the laces on his boots, yanks them off and removes his socks. 'Can you stand?'

'I think so.'

He struggles to his feet, and she offers the flask again.

'I'm sorry,' he says, in-between gulps of water. 'I don't know—'

She kisses his wet lips. 'It's not far now.'

*

They reach the boardwalk leading to the jetty.

'Bring the crystal,' says the woman, before striding across the boards.

Mary goes to follow but jumps back onto the sand. 'Too hot,' she says, ramming her sandals back on her feet.

Rico sits and pulls his socks and shoes back on, looking along the beach. 'I shan't be sorry to get out of here.' He stands, unties the bag containing the crystal and removes it from Wanita's saddle.

'Here's the boat,' says Mary, pointing out to sea.

A white wooden dinghy hums towards them, a man at the rear working the outboard motor with one hand. Behind him, the horizon boat has anchored, pausing its up and down journey.

Mary steps onto the boards again. 'Wow,' she says, looking down at the sea.

Rico joins her and they watch shoals of parrot fish dart backwards and forwards, chasing silver tiddlers, who jump in and out of the water to escape their pursuers. The only noise comes from the boat hum and the waves hitting the tubular steel supports holding up the boardwalk. Suddenly, a galaxy of starfish – pink, purple and blue – appear from nowhere, dancing through the water.

'You know they're basically a walking head,' says Rico.

'Are you sure?' says Mary, laughing.

'Absolutely. And they regenerate, grow a new arm if necessary. Look at their sparkles. It's like they've been sprinkled.'

The starfish sway, turn as one and head out into the ocean.

'This place could be idyllic,' says Rico.

Mary kisses Wanita's nose and ties a waterbag round her neck. 'Wait here, old girl. We'll not be long.'

The camel grunts, drops her head and drinks.

'The boat's nearly here,' shouts the woman. 'You need to hurry.'

They pace along the boards, reach the steps into

the water, where she's waiting, and watch as the boatman surges the engine and comes alongside. He throws a rope, which the woman grabs and ties to a mooring post.

'Are you ready?' shouts the man.

'Get in the boat,' says the woman.

'I thought he was bringing the second crystal,' says Mary.

'You have to leave. He has the crystal safe.'

'I need to get my camel.'

'The camel stays,' says the woman, nodding towards the beach.

'Look,' says Rico. 'Behind Wanita.'

Two men, bare legs; buffed, tanned leather panels clinging to their torsos. One of them points to the boat; the other pats the camel's back.

'Jinga,' says Mary. 'I can't leave her.'

'You've no choice,' says the woman. 'She'll not be hurt, and you'll see her again.'

Mary's stomach twists and cramps, and a sob escapes her mouth.

'We'll get her back,' says Rico, pulling her close.

'The Jinga can't follow the boat,' says the woman, 'but they'll track you in your next destination. And now you must go.'

Mary takes a few steps towards the beach.

The Jinga pats the camel again and runs a hand across his throat.

'I'm coming back for you,' shouts Mary, before turning to the woman. 'You guarantee she'll be safe.'

'Harming the camel is not part of their orders.'

Mary looks again at the beach.

Rico takes her arm. 'Come on. The quicker we get the crystals, the earlier you'll get her back.'

They turn and climb down the steps into the boat.

*

Mary stares at the receding beach as they hum their way towards the chug boat, which is anchored on the horizon. She sees the woman walk back along the boards and the Jinga head away, leaving Wanita drinking from her waterbag. The woman reaches her, and Mary feels a leaden weight lift from her shoulders when she gently strokes the camel's head and takes her reins.

'She'll be fine,' says Rico, pushing the crystal between his legs.

'I need to find a way back to her,' says Mary.

Rico pulls her to him and glares at the man steering the boat. T-shirt and shorts; thick, black hair; a Tom Selleck moustache. 'You've got the crystal?'

The boatman gives them a hard look and surges the engine.

'I guess that's a yes,' says Mary, wiping her eyes.

They sit in silence as the horizon chug boat gets

closer and closer. A puff of breeze tugs at their hair and a sprinkle of sea spray washes their faces as they cut through the waves. Fruit bats screech overhead, heading towards a different shore.

Mary registers for the first time that the beach they've left is part of an island, with other islands plopped in the ocean around them. An archipelago nestling in a turquoise sea. 'You're right. This place could be idyllic. Are you okay now?'

'I never want to be back there again,' he says.

They reach the chug boat, and a smell of diesel hits their nostrils as they bob up and down on the water. The boatman manoeuvres the dinghy alongside the steps. 'Wait here,' he snarls, climbing the ladder.

'I thought we were coming with you,' says Rico.

The boatman ignores him, drops onto the deck above them and then reappears holding a sack secured to a rope. 'Here's your crystal,' he shouts, lowering it to the dinghy. 'Now go.'

The sack lands; Rico unties the rope, opens it and brings a second piece of labradorite into the sun. The same amber translucence and pulsating veins, but this time a square block, about the size of its football companion. Mary fetches the first one from its bag and sits the crystals side by side on the wooden deck.

'They look like they belong together,' says Rico. 'Just one to go.'

The chug boat moves away, churning the sea, sploshing waves into the dinghy as they sit stranded in the middle of the ocean. They see the boatman behind the wheel, steering his ship towards the horizon. 'Where are you going?' shouts Mary. 'What happens to us?'

'Change of plan, I'm afraid.'

'Jethro,' says Rico, smiling at the smoke human, who hovers over the water. 'Are we glad to see you.'

'Wanita,' says Mary. 'I need to know she's okay.'

'The princess has her,' says Jethro, beaming his bad teeth. 'The Jinga have presented a problem, though.'

'They've tracked us,' says Rico. 'I thought Fats taking the ring would distract them.'

'A second tracker,' says Jethro. 'A memory stick.'

Mary fetches it from her pocket. 'I didn't know it—'

'We must move you. You'll be safer in your hometown, with other people. The princess has sent you a gift.'

He silently clicks his smoky fingers, and a silver fob watch materialises on the deck.

Rico picks it up and flicks open the cover.

Red digits counting down the time.

13:58; 13:57…

'You're nearly halfway,' says Jethro, clicking his fingers again. Two backpacks appear next to the crystals. 'You'll need these. There's a change of clothes inside.'

153

Mary holds up the memory stick. 'What shall I do with this?'

'It's up to you. It might delay the Jinga if you don't have it, but the emperor knows where you're heading.'

She looks at Rico. 'You promise to tell me everything when we're safe.'

'I promise,' he says.

She hurls the memory stick into the sea.

XLVIII

Livia runs her hand over the plasma pool and closes the image of an embracing Rico and Mary bobbing up and down in a wooden dinghy. She walks over to the window of the atrium and gazes at a gas planet with rainbow rings and sparkling ice moons rolling by. *Tempting*, she tells herself, a nice addition for the empire, but she knows its air is sulphurous, even to gods, and its only purpose is to serve as a decoration in the sky – like a bauble on a Christmas tree.

She turns towards the teller sisters, Paloma and Sini, who spin and weave at their loom, endlessly casting stories. 'Why didn't we realise the memory stick could be traced?'

'It didn't appear in the fates,' says Paloma, stretching her emaciated body towards the glass ceiling.

'Perhaps the loom sets false trails,' says Sebastian, who is standing at the back of the atrium. 'The emperor has already—'

'Yes,' says Livia, silencing him by holding up her hand. She looks again at the pool. 'My champion and his girl seem happy. I'm regretting taking the ring away.'

'Your rationale was sensible,' says Sebastian, coming to her side, 'but you think the ring might work now?'

'What do the fates tell us?' she says, nodding at the sisters. 'Are they destined?'

'The weave isn't clear,' says Paloma. 'Do you want us to unpick and spin again?'

'We need to know. I'm assuming the gangster can be redirected.'

'The ring can be returned,' says Sebastian, 'but maybe that's premature. Your champion has two crystals; the gangster is still free; and time ticks by on the emperor.'

'There's still plenty of time. Is the gangster still of interest?'

'The emperor wants the ring, Your Highness. A Jinga lieutenant has been dispatched in pursuit.' He hesitates. 'And there's something else. Your father has summoned the monk.'

'Bernard. Why?'

'He's been seen talking with the smoke humans.'

She looks at the sisters. 'They appeared on the loom, and now Bernard talks to them. I don't understand. Is there something I'm missing, perhaps in your weave?'

Paloma shakes her head.

'Bring the smoke humans to me at once. I need to question them myself.'

Sebastian walks quickly out of the atrium.

Livia slumps on her throne. Bernard. The only thing she has left of Helena, now she's estranged from Octavius. An image from childhood comes back to her: cuddling through the night in front of a log fire in a fairy wood; listening to folk tales of old empires and love stories of the gods; fireflies dancing in her hair; Bernard barbequing meat and topping up her mother's wine goblet. Lots of laughing; lots of love. Family. But there's something else, lingering on the edge of memory, just out of reach. So long ago, but having him here has maintained a connection, given her someone to talk to about her mother, but now he meets with the smoke humans behind her back and has been summoned by Octavius. 'You said before the empress might return.'

'A feeling,' says Sini. 'Anything is possible.'

'Spin again and ask that question.'

'The emperor may not—'

'Let me worry about the emperor.'

The teller sisters look at each other. 'As you wish,' says Paloma.

XLIX

Fats grabs a seat halfway along the upper deck of the night bus and thanks God he's the only one there. A nauseating smell of woodbines, piss and kebabs makes him check the window, but it's already slid open to its max. It astonishes him that the council, with all its cutbacks, runs a round-the-town bus service after midnight, but he has a theory that it's a cheap form of community service – a refuge for the nutters and crackheads to call home. The lower deck is a favourite. Warmer and less of a stench, but he needs the isolation and time to think.

Misty drizzle shows up under the street lights as the high street rolls past. He mentally ticks off the properties. Charity shops, laundrettes, nail bars and, slap in the middle, an oasis of waterside apartments with arch, leaded windows overlooking the river. He still doesn't get why anyone with money would want to live there. With that kind of cash, he'd move uptown, near the bistros and fashion boutiques, but he guesses it's part of a long game, a takeover, the locals boarding up their spaces and filling their boots with yellow-brick-road money, seduced by estate agents and property developers. It'll soon be complete, a rich man's ghetto, but, for now, a strange fruit of shithole and cash means opportunity for the likes of Jean and her protection posse.

Someone rings the bell.

The bus hisses to a stop; the opening whoosh of the door drifts to the upper deck. Adrenalin stirs in his veins as he watches the stairs, ready to fight or flight. He relaxes as they pull away from the kerb, searches his head for the tune his dad used to sing. Ian Dury's 'Apples'. The street drifts by once more, a cardboard city tenant huddling in every doorway – sleeping bags for lucky hoboes, given out for an expected thank you by County Hall in place of real houses. Sensible street sleepers wait to get their heads down, let the nightclub drunks pass through, unless they want a kicking from a wasted no-mark looking for someone to blame for a shit life.

He stares at his reflection in the window. Hair scrunched tight in a ponytail; donkey jacket collar turned up. He hates his puffy eyes, and his lips have a blue tinge, but he doesn't look bad for a bloke who snuffed it a couple of days ago. He touches the ring and wonders how the champion and his girl are getting on with the map. At least they're not being chased by a demented warrior from the afterlife. That bloke in the pub looked normal enough, apart from the holes each side of his nostrils, but his cold eyes gave it away. The dead stare of a killer. It takes one to know one. At least he'd taken out the hoop ring, but who the fuck told him to wear a trilby? He grins and hopes the barman stung a big tip from the credit card.

'How's it going, buddy?'

He turns his head towards the voice.

The albino smiles at him from the back seat. 'You don't look pleased to see me.'

'It's been a long day,' says Fats.

'You've done well. Not many escape the Jinga.'

'I got lucky. I'm guessing hoop man is still chasing me.'

'You still have the ring. I expected you to dump it.'

'No point. You seem to be holding all the cards.'

The albino laughs, showing off his protracted incisors, which drip dread down Fats' spine. Just when he thought this guy couldn't get any creepier.

Sebastian walks up the bus and sits next to him.

'I'm guessing this isn't a social call,' says Fats.

'A change of plan. You're to return the ring. The champion and his girl may still have use for it.'

'You mean they're in danger from these Jinga guys?'

'The princess feels the ring may help them escape.'

'And what about me?'

'You'll take the crystals and set a false trail. The Jinga will come after you—'

'And eventually catch me.'

'That's your job, or maybe that's slipped your mind.'

'It doesn't look like I have a choice.'

'No,' says Sebastian, reaching in his pocket and handing Fats a folded piece of paper. 'Here's their location. They don't know you're coming. You'll have to explain.'

Fats takes the paper and stares out the window. It's still raining, and the bus has turned back on itself, heading along the opposite side of the high street.

'You look homesick,' says Sebastian.

'Not really. Never had one to miss.'

'Do your job well and the princess will reward you.'

With a final grin, and without a word of goodbye, the albino stands, strides along the upper deck and disappears down the stairs, the manservant's bell push stopping the bus like every other punter.

Fats turns the paper over in his hand and looks through the window as Sebastian lands on the pavement. 'Think. There must be something.'

The bus pulls away and he looks back at a desolate street, the albino having disappeared into the night-time drizzle. 'Of course he has,' Fats mutters to himself. 'You can't expect an agent of God to get a fucking taxi.'

He checks the address on the paper.

A bookshop in the centre of town.

Get the ring back. They must be confident it'll work, and then he'll be left with all the killers on his back. 'Think,' he says again, punching his thigh to try and focus his mind. He glances round the upper deck, grateful there's no one there to judge and label him a nutter. He punches himself one more time, harder. The pain makes him bite his lip and wince.

'...the princess will reward you.'

The albino's words circle his head, but he doesn't believe them. He's on his own. Same as it ever was. Being in Jean's posse meant staying two streets ahead of everyone, protecting his own skin. There must be... He remembers the crystals, the map. An escape route with a vacancy if the champion is out of the picture. He touches the ring. 'Time to get you home.'

He stands and pushes the bell.

L

Underneath the games room glass floor of Octavius's starship, a black hole fires hot plasma into space, whilst its gas rings circle a pit of nothingness. Getting too close to its no-return gravitational suck makes even gods nervous, but, for Octavius, hovering here over a game of chess adds jeopardy and makes him feel alive.

He moves his white knight two squares vertically and one square horizontally. 'Check,' he says, glee filling his voice. 'You're done for, Captain.'

The Jinga contemplates the board, sees an obvious escape but also notices the emperor yawning, a signal Octavius has hit boredom threshold. He nervously glances between his feet. The order to shift orbit away from the miniscule margin for error will come soon, meaning the entire crew can breathe again. Every nanosecond brings a risk of being grabbed into an abyss. It all adds to the captain's list of concerns about the emperor's state of mind. He shifts his king and waits for the inevitable.

'Checkmate,' says Octavius, pushing his queen diagonally.

'Well done, Your Majesty. Three games in a row.'

Octavius slides the board away and stands. 'Enough, for now,' he says, staring at the black hole. 'It's time we moved our position.'

The captain comes to his side as another gush of plasma shoots by the starship. 'It's very beautiful. Is nothing known of life beyond its surface?'

'No one has ever come back to tell the story, but gossip keeps even my brother, Wrath, awake. Move us. We've had our adventure.'

'At once. Shall I send in the monk?'

'Yes,' says Octavius, smiling. 'Let him see the black hole. A reminder of where he can be dropped.'

The captain nods and leaves the room.

A new rocket of plasma flashes by.

'At least you're not in there, my darling,' whispers Octavius.

He turns to the sound of a door opening behind him. 'Bernard,' he says, holding out his arms, 'come and join me.'

'Your Majesty,' says Bernard, taking off his cassock hood and striding across the floor, 'I must protest—'

'Protest?' says Octavius, dropping his embrace.

'The way I've been brought here, like a common criminal. I'm a member of the ecclesia—'

'Have you seen the view?' says Octavius, putting

his hand on Bernard's shoulder and guiding him to his side.

'A black hole,' says Bernard, taking a hard swallow.

'Isn't it wonderful? Existing to consume anything crossing its path. Now, that's power. You look nervous. We're perfectly safe.'

'Should we be this close?'

Another plasma gush makes Bernard flinch.

Octavius laughs. 'Look at it, gobbling everything. Imagine being dropped into its clutches. Not even an ecclesia member would survive.'

Bernard stares at the pit. He feels Octavius's grip on his shoulder tighten as they watch in silence. His scar throbs, a warning sign his body has perfected over the years. He looks at Octavius, who smiles at him.

'Shall we sit, Bernard?'

'Of course. Is there anything in—'

'I want to talk to you about Helena.'

The door opens and clicks shut as the Jinga captain takes his place in the shadows.

'Do you play?' says Octavius, waving his hand towards the table.

'A little,' says Bernard, taking in the played-out chess game. 'It looks like a close contest.'

Octavius leans forward and lowers his voice. 'My captain lets me win, but I understand. Everyone fears the consequence of my defeat. The only time gods have genuine games is when playing fellow gods. Is that not so?'

'A match of equals, Your Highness.'

'Which brings me to Helena,' says Octavius, lifting his voice to a normal level. 'You recall the card game with my brother?'

'Most unfortunate, and with tragic—'

'Nothing should have gone wrong. My pack, shuffler, dealer, and I'm an excellent card player.'

'But you punished my brothers—'

'On your guidance, and they exist in smoke form now, while you're a member of the ecclesia.'

'Your generosity is—'

'Tell me again why you think them responsible for Helena's fate.'

Bernard glances towards the door. He hears the Jinga take a deep breath. 'It must have been one of them. They were the only ones in contact with the pack.'

'But that's not true. They handled the pack on the day of the game, but you brought the cards.'

'They were sealed when I delivered them.'

Octavius sits in one of the chairs and gestures to the other.

'Do you suspect me of something?' says Bernard, taking a seat.

'You've become very close to Livia.'

'Her Highness seeks my guidance. I am family.'

'You're advising her?'

'I help in whatever way I can, but I'd do the same for you.'

'Very well. What do you know about her champion?'

Bernard looks again at the chessboard and then out of the window, trying to calculate his words. The black hole gets smaller and smaller as the starship moves through the gears and retreats to a safe distance. 'The princess has recruited a gangster, to set a false trail, away from the champion.'

'Tell me something I don't know, Captain. Our friend wants to revisit the black hole and take a closer look.'

'The champion has two crystals,' splutters Bernard. 'He searches for the third.'

'She sends them to the well?'

'I think so.'

'But the gangster has the ring?'

'He does.'

Octavius watches the black hole disappear. 'You have many friends, Bernard. From your position on the ecclesia, you mix with the great and the good.'

'I've been fortunate.'

'And I've made you immortal, but that can be changed. Remember, I decide your fate. Now go, but keep me informed.'

*

Bernard closes the games room door, reaches into his cassock, fetches out a handkerchief and wipes his face. His cheek scar still throbs, and he wonders why the emperor asks questions now about a card game that has become a fog in most memories. And then the detail about the champion and the princess. It feels wrong, like he's missing a critical piece of jigsaw.

He shudders at the emperor's threats and follows the captain along a corridor, heading back to the Jinga transport ship that awaits him. The thought of the black hole makes him quicken his stride, eager to return home and think through what has happened, have a word with ecclesia colleagues. Talk to the princess.

The captain stops and opens a door leading off the corridor and into a small office. 'May I have a word?'

Bernard hesitates, conscious he's with a Jinga captain. He looks into the room. Innocent enough. 'Of course.'

The captain closes the door behind them, and they face each other in a windowless space, no furniture, just a few boxes stacked in one corner and a musty smell. 'How do you feel your meeting with the emperor went?'

'What do you mean?' says Bernard.

'Do you feel it went well?'

'I don't understand. Was the emperor not happy with me?'

'I'm asking your opinion.'

The throbs from Bernard's scar increase, like a heart stimulated by an electric probe. His mind tells him to be careful; this could be a trap. No Jinga has ever asked questions of this sort. 'You'll have to be more specific.'

'Do you think the emperor's behaviour rational?'

'Do you?'

The captain touches the hilt of his sword. 'I have my worries.'

'You think the emperor unwell.'

'He grieves for the empress.'

'Surely, that's normal, after what happened.'

'I wonder if you plan on talking to the princess.'

Bernard meets the captain's eyes. He can't believe what he's hearing, but the implication seems obvious. His head races with jeopardy. It could be the emperor testing his loyalty after their last exchange. The image of the black hole comes back into his head. 'About what?'

'Concerns for the emperor.'

Still no indication of the right answer. Deliberate, or is the Jinga feeling for safe passage? The risks from this conversation run both ways. 'Are you saying you have concerns?'

'We all do,' says the captain.

'And you think I should talk to the princess?'

'My concern is for the emperor, and I thought, with you being a member of the ecclesia, you'd know how best to proceed.'

'I see,' says Bernard, trying to read the captain's face, but there's no clues apart from a slight twitch at the corner of his mouth. A tell of a trap or a nervousness of action? It could be either. 'Leave it with me, but I'm sure the emperor is well.'

LI

Jethro looks at his bobbing smoky brothers as they wait for Livia to take her throne. They all stare back expectantly, and he forces himself to drop the tension in his face and smile. The pressure to keep them well can be overwhelming. He's not worried about the twins. They've been easy enough to control, ever since their mum died, but Michael has a maverick mouth and can be unpredictable. He's told him to be quiet, leave him to do the talking; reassured them all that a regular update is part of the brief, so the albino's summons is not unusual. But Jethro expected just him, and the mood feels different this time. A stiffness of anger in the princess's body; a sliver of ice in the air. He tells himself to tread softly.

Livia registers them one by one. 'Sebastian tells me you've been meeting with my uncle.'

'You mean the monk?' says Jethro.

'You know I do. And don't forget your manners, human.'

'Apologies, Your Highness. I was surprised by your question. I expected to be giving an update on the game.'

'And you will, but first tell me about my uncle.'

'He takes an interest in our fate,' says Michael, grinning.

'Forgive my brother,' says Jethro, his heartbeat quickening. 'He means the monk seeks our foretelling guidance. We descend from gypsies; our mother was known for her prophecy skills.'

'You're soothsayers?'

'We have the genes.'

'And Bernard is a believer?'

'He comes to us occasionally.'

'My fates have never mentioned you. They know all the prophets in my empire.'

'We're strictly a family firm,' says Michael.

Jethro glares at him and Michael drops his eyes.

'You,' says Livia, pointing at Michael, 'tell me what's going on.'

'I speak for all of us,' says Jethro.

Livia gestures towards Sebastian. 'Extinguish the twins. Maybe that will get the truth out of them.'

'Your Highness,' protests Jethro.

'You told me once being snuffed out would be a relief. Tell me, or I'll take away their existence.'

Jethro looks again along the line of his brothers.

Michael lifts his head, goes to speak but says nothing.

'Do it,' says Livia.

Sebastian roots himself underneath the twins and raises his hands. Alfie and Thomas scream as he grabs their smoke plumes, plaits their gaseous bodies and guides them towards the pool.

'They will die,' says Livia, 'unless I hear the truth.'

More screams as Sebastian lowers his prey closer to the bubbling plasma.

'He's family,' blurts out Michael.

Livia claps her hands.

Sebastian releases his grip, letting the twins float to their original positions.

'Family,' says Livia. 'How can that be possible?'

'Our half-brother,' says Jethro.

'But that means... why have I no knowledge of you?'

'The emperor destroyed your memory.'

'Then why would you not tell me? Surely, it's to your advantage.'

Jethro looks at Sebastian. 'He'll probably drop us in the pool when we do, but maybe you'll listen to our side of the story first.'

LII

Octavius clears the plasma vision of Fats stepping away from the night bus and turns towards his captain. 'The gangster is clever.'

'The ring tells us his exact location, sir.'

'And yet, he evaded your lieutenant.'

'A lucky break. Shall we pick him up?'

Penelope screeches from her cage. Octavius walks over and rattles lightly across the bars. She sidles towards him, blinks once and nuzzles his inserted fingers. 'My harpy looks better since Cicero's seed mix. Don't you think?'

'Much better,' says the captain, 'but what shall we do with the human?'

'The woman never read my memory stick?'

'Our sensors say it remains unopened, and it looks like it's been destroyed.'

'Despite my warnings, she's still with her champion. Humans and their love instinct. Helena would have forgiven me anything.'

The captain waits, not knowing how to respond.

Octavius kisses Penelope's beak through the bars. The harpy meets his eyes and whispers, 'She loves you. You need to get her back.'

'I know,' mouths Octavius.

A cough from the captain.

'Let the human have his fun,' says Octavius. 'We know where he's heading. Your precious Jinga can catch him the old-fashioned way. Is that a problem?'

'No, sir. You mean ignore the ring—'

'I still want the ring, but switch off the tracker. I want Livia to have a sporting chance of success.'

'At once,' says the captain, marching out of the room.

The emperor turns back towards the birdcage. 'The power of soulmates,' he mutters, 'it can't be ignored.'

Penelope nuzzles his fingers again.

LIII

The pavement café has barely warmed up its tables, but it already has three customers working their way through a large cafetiere of Jamaica blue coffee.

Grace, the café owner, watches them from behind the counter. She's taken payment upfront. Not something she does with her regulars, likes to leave an open bill in case they're tempted to buy more, but she calculates these guys, huddled together like they're plotting, are well capable of doing a runner. And they don't look comfortable in their own skin. They're wearing brown trench coats, hoop rings through their noses and a glare to stop traffic. Stereotype Mafioso, which would be hysterical if it wasn't for the dead eyes the one in the middle seat gave her, sending a surge of fear through her body. She looks at the clock on the wall. Half an hour before greasy Joe, the cook, gets here. Meantime, she'll stay behind the counter and watch from a distance.

A diesel black cab belches by, making Augustus, one of the Jinga warriors, cough. 'The woman watches us,' he says, wiping his mouth.

'Ignore her,' says Hector, taking a sip of his coffee. 'The humans head for the bookshop. We need to capture them quickly and get them to the emperor. They can be destroyed, if necessary, but any disruption on the planet needs to be kept to a minimum. Corpses return with us.'

Augustus coughs again, pours himself a glass of water and takes a slurp. 'The two from the boat are sentimental. I thought the girl would give herself up for the camel.'

'We should have cut its throat,' says Anthony, the other warrior.

'Killing camels isn't in our orders,' says Hector. 'There's one more thing. We need to make sure the ring is brought to the emperor.'

'The ring?'

'Do you have a problem with that, Augustus?'

'No, sir. It's just not—'

'The emperor wants the ring. And be careful with the gangster. He's sharp.'

'The waitress is on her way,' says Anthony.

'Can I get you gentlemen anything else?' says Grace, hovering nervously in the café doorway.

Hector stands and the warriors follow suit. 'Nothing,' he snarls, and all three men stride away down the street.

Grace watches them go, hoping they never darken her door again.

LIV

Livia strokes the edge of the loom, conscious of Sini and Paloma's eyes on her back, waiting for her to say something. The smoke humans have been dismissed under a strict oath of silence, but they've told their card story: how Helena begged for their lives and then Octavius wiped Livia's memory of their existence, leaving just Bernard – a half-brother – as her only blood. Her instinct is to restore their form, bring them back to her, but she knows it's Octavius's curse to break.

She glares at the sisters. 'How many people know?'

'It's so long ago,' says Paloma, 'and the emperor banished any talk.'

'There can't have been many,' says Sebastian. 'Just those in close contact with the ecclesia and distanced from you.'

'I suppose it suited his purpose to isolate me, but why not wipe my memory of the game as well? It doesn't make any sense.'

Paloma looks at Sini and then back at Livia. 'He was grieving—'

'For what? His foolish risk sealed my mother's fate.'

'The monk has known the truth all along,' says Sebastian, coming to her side.

'My half-uncle,' spits Livia, looking again at the loom. 'And now he plots with Octavius.'

'We don't know that for certain,' says Sini. 'He could still be on your side.'

'It's that naivety he's relied on for years.'

Sebastian nods. 'The empress was brave, Your Highness, to think of her siblings whilst being taken away by Wrath.'

Livia walks over to the window and stares at Earth. 'My mother's homeland. It draws me every time we pass.'

'It runs in your veins,' says Sini.

'Octavius thinks it makes me weak, but he's wrong.'

'Shall I fetch the monk?' says Sebastian.

'We'll deal with him later. Concentrate on the game and get me an audience with the ecclesia. It's time I updated them on our progress.'

*

Back in the sanctuary, the orb blinks out its purple rhythm in silence, waiting for Livia to speak.

179

She stretches out on a couch in her private lounge, next to her gym, and stares up at the dreamcatchers floating above her head. Circular webs fluttering in the draught, they're replenished every morning by the worker spiders that live in the corners of the atrium – another ever-present legacy from her mother. 'They'll catch the bad dreams before they reach you, sweetheart.' An image of Beelzebub flashes to the front of her mind. 'Another lie,' she mutters.

'Nothing is foolproof,' says the orb. 'What troubles you?'

Sitting up, she turns off the couch and stares incredulously at the orb levitating in front of her. 'Seriously?'

'You seem angry.'

'I don't understand why he'd do that. Why wipe my memory of them?'

'I can only make a guess,' says the orb, drifting closer.

She stands, pulls down the coat of her pinstripe suit, fastens the top button, starts to walk towards the door but stops and looks at the orb again – Helena's face smiling at her through fizzing sparkles. 'Sometimes, I forget she's not here.'

'Your father knew I'd bring you comfort.'

'There you go again, taking his side. Has he programmed you to twist my thoughts? I had to find out about the smoke humans from them. Aren't you meant to speak the truth?'

'I didn't—'

'If you're going to say you didn't know, I find that hard to believe. Very well, tell me your guess.'

'He wiped your memory of their existence to deny them, even in smoke form, the privilege of being your family. That's also why he banished any talk.'

'So, it's all about punishing the humans. Nothing to do with me. Is that the best you can do?'

'He had to do something, and the loss of your uncles was the least intrusive option. He left your memory of the card game because he couldn't deny you the truth about Helena's disappearance, even if it meant cursing himself with your anger.'

Livia rolls her eyes and looks up at the dreamcatchers. 'You make him sound like a saint. He gambled with my mother's life. That tells me everything I need to know.'

And with that, she walks out of the lounge, slamming the door behind her.

The orb blinks into the empty room. 'No one is a saint,' it whispers. 'You'll find that out soon enough.'

*

From her platinum throne, Livia waits impatiently for the opening festivities of an ecclesia gathering to be over. All she wants is to meet with the gods left by Octavius to guide and advise her reign, but she must follow protocols and traditions, which includes the nonsense now being played out in front of her.

She surveys the crowd as they sate their appetite for food from a bustling street market. High-ranking officials who have served for millennia mixing with lowly bureaucrats on a break from their paperclip responsibilities in provincial town halls; minstrels in rainbow-coloured suits plucking away at harps and sitars, backdropped by a Ferris wheel driven by fairies with sparkling wands. Laughter hums in every corner, reverberating off the glass walls and ceiling.

Tired and feeling as though enough time has been wasted, she stands and claps once in the direction of a muscle man clothed in a loin cloth. He swings a brass striker round his head and connects with a bronze shield. 'Let the formalities commence,' he bellows.

A hush falls on the atrium; the snack stalls bang their shutters down; and the musicians come to a silent stop. The crowd parts, creating a smoky walkway from the back of the room, and a trumpeter marches through, comes to a halt in front of the stage and blows a fanfare. Livia claps again, triggering a single strike of the gong, making everyone turn towards the atrium's entrance doors for the arrival of the ecclesia.

The first to appear is Timus, God of Strategy. He plods along the walkway like a polar bear in a toga candida, rubbing enthusiastically at his pot belly and heading towards Livia and the line of vacant chaise longues next to her throne. A thin smile trickles across his lips, but she knows his darting eyes reveal a vengeful paranoia, ready to ignite his ranting rages. A jealous lover who bullies young men – God or human – into submission, she's lost count of the number of times in her short reign she's had to intervene to stop him murdering them when his lust has been spent.

The gong strikes again and this time two goshawks swoop into the room, weave round the ceiling and land on the shoulders of the next god to take the walkway. Phillippa, God of Fates, pulls her lion-skin coat tight and strides her path towards the stage. She whispers something to each of the birds, who nibble at her neck in reply, and then she waves to the crowd, theatrical style, like she's the one they've all come to see – the star of the show. Her gentle, grey eyes sparkle as her mere presence whips the crowd into a frenzy and she gets close enough for eye contact with Livia, who can't help but smile at such a grand entrance.

Another strike.

Livia raises her eyes to the ceiling, knowing full well which god is next to appear. Darius, God of Messages, flutters into the room, propelled by his winged feet, like a song thrush launched into a party. His cherub face is covered in a smattering of freckles; long blond hair trails behind him as he glides towards the stage, beaming white teeth and choirboy eyes. Livia looks at Timus, who has reached the chaise longues and is now, as she knew he would, lusting his gaze in Darius's direction. The thought makes her feel slightly nauseous and she forces herself to turn again towards the atrium's doors.

A final gong sounds, and she takes a deep breath.

The crowd gasps as Athos, God of War, enters the atrium. Out of respect, he's ditched the battle dress suction panels that normally adorn his body and opted for a toga palmata – reserved for use by the highest-ranking, conquering generals. Made from the wool of moon alpacas, dyed purple and decorated with gold palm branches, it looks like someone has casually thrown it round his muscular frame and pinned it in place with a spitting cobra brooch. His bare arms, shoulders and calf muscles remind Livia of the legend that says his body is carved from marble. She feels a drop in the pit of her stomach as he gets closer. Thick, luscious lips; blue eyes that look like they can see into your soul; a god who can adjust his height to suit the occasion, towering cliffs if need be. He smiles at her, only her, his gaze never shifting from her face as he marches towards the stage. She remembers his compassion when she was a child, and he'd take his turn at minding the emperor's daughter. And then she grew up and noticed his interest change. How she wishes it were possible.

The trumpeter blows a closing fanfare.

'Ecclesia,' says Livia, brushing the thought of Athos from her mind and coming back into the room with a start. She gestures towards the gold chaise longues.

They walk slowly onto the stage, each collecting a goblet of wine from two bare-chested male waiters. Timus speaks to one of them and Livia thinks about intervening but stops herself. Riling Timus before the meeting starts would not be smart.

The crowd files slowly out of the atrium, leaving the ecclesia to their business, heavy doors banging shut, the sound echoing round the chamber. 'My ecclesia,' says Livia, taking her seat. 'I want to—'

'We've heard about your game with the emperor,' says Timus.

She fixes him with a stare. 'You interrupt me, Timus.'

A flash of irritation ghosts Timus's face. He looks at his fellow gods for support, but none meet his eyes. 'My apologies,' he says, resting his hands on his belly.

'Should we not wait for the human?' says Phillippa.

Everyone's eyes fall on the vacant chaise longue.

Livia brushes a speck of dust from the arm of her pinstripe suit. 'The monk visits the emperor. And he's already aware of the update.'

'You've spoken to him before us.'

'No, Timus. The emperor has updated him.'

'Outrageous. He's not even a god—'

'For heaven's sake,' says Athos, 'let the princess speak. You'll have your turn soon enough.'

The gods adjust their lying position and take a sip of wine.

Livia glares at Timus before continuing.

LV

Rico stands in the unlit tobacconist shop doorway, turning over the silver fob watch Jethro gave them to track the game countdown. Two hours of wasted time, afternoon morphing into dusk while they circled town to find the third crystal's location. He looks at the building opposite – dirty grey net curtains, a mass of dead flies in the shop window. 'Looks like the owner did a runner years ago,' he says, shaking his head.

Mary, now dressed in jeans, hoodie and Nike trainers, holds the map in front of her, bending it slightly so it catches the beam from the street light. 'This is definitely it. Look, above the door, *Billy's Books*.'

A BMW slides past, and they step back into the shadows.

'I feel like we're being watched,' she says. 'Do you think they're here?'

'Jethro said they know the location. So, I'm guessing, yes. Is there any point if the Jinga know where we are?'

'What choice do we have? We'll figure it out as we go.'

They adjust their backpacks, race across the road and down an alley at the side of the bookshop. Rico crouches next to a garden wall, interlocks his fingers and looks at Mary.

'What?' she says.

'Up you go. See if there's any activity.'

'Thanks, Champ.'

'It makes sense. You'll never take my weight.'

She puts a foot into his cupped hands, pulls herself onto the wall and scans the back of the property.

'What can you see?'

'Nothing. Total darkness. We should have got here during opening hours.'

'Pull me up. There must be a way in.'

He jumps halfway up the wall and grabs the top with his free hand. She pulls at his arms as he tries to scramble up the moss-covered bricks. With a grunt, he slides back down. A loose piece of mortar drops into the alley, triggering a dog bark in the distance. They shoot a look at the house and then towards the street.

'It's no good,' she says. 'You're too heavy.'

'Now what do we do?' he says.

She scans the alley. 'That wheelie bin. Climb on top of it.'

He pushes the green bin against the wall, jumps

onto its lid and pulls himself up alongside Mary. 'Pity you didn't think of that before.'

She gives him a hard stare and then looks again at the house. 'No sign of life. Perhaps they're concentrating on Fats. Do you think they'll chase him, now they know where we're heading?'

'Probably. The Jinga aren't known for loose ends.' He hangs from the top of the wall, releases his grip and lands on a lawn. 'We need to concentrate on the crystal, and the princess says it's in that bookshop. Come on.'

She lowers herself into his arms and they edge their way towards the back door.

LVI

A gong chimes round the atrium to signal a break in proceedings.

Livia feels the weight of her thirty minutes sparring with Timus and the forensic grilling by Phillippa, but she knows the update is necessary to keep the ecclesia, at least openly, on her side. She stands and watches the atrium return to its hustle and bustle – food shutters clattering open; fairies rolling the Ferris wheel back to life; musicians plucking once more at their strings; and a chattering crowd flocking through the now open doors.

Another chime brings a smoke-filled olive jar from the ceiling, iron chains swinging it over an empty stage. Inside, two humans, a man and a woman, rise from a garden swing, an invisible puppeteer moving their string-attached limbs in a ghostly waltz, frosty smoke accentuating a slow-motion dance.

'You're not happy, Princess?'

'Athos,' she says, turning towards the warrior, who

has kept his body at the height of his host, 'I thought you'd left for refreshment.'

'No need. I'll let Timus have my share. You look sad.'

'I wish we didn't have to mock humans,' she says, nodding at the olive jar dancers.

'Harmless fun. Though I understand the sensitivity to your mother's species.'

'My sensitivity is to how it reflects on gods. Nothing more.'

'You think it shows us in a bad way.'

'It's cruel and unnecessary, but Octavius's traditions persist.'

'Maybe you're right, but change happening too quickly makes—'

'I know, Athos,' she says, holding up her hand. 'I've learnt the sensitivities off by heart.' She goes to walk away, but he touches her shoulder, making her stop and look at him.

'You sound frustrated,' he says, 'and yet you persist with this game. Is that necessary?'

'I have no choice. The emperor likes his distractions.'

'Your champion means a lot to you. Maybe you show a weakness.'

'No more than you for the warrior Achilles, or Phillippa for her goshawks.'

He laughs and holds out his arm. 'Fair enough.

And you're right. It is all a game. Shall we get some refreshment?'

'Should you be consorting with a half-human?'

'Maybe it's you who resists the arm of a god. I'm hoping that's not how you judge me.'

She smiles and takes his arm, noting the playful gleam in the warrior's eyes. 'I don't think a goblet of wine will bring the universe crashing down.'

LVII

Anthony watches the two humans creep towards the house. He turns from his crouching position beneath the shed window. 'Just as you said, sir. They've arrived for the crystal.'

Hector takes a draw on his cigarette, a pack given to him by the captain as part of his disguise. Glowing ash momentarily lights up his face. 'We need to be patient, wait for the gangster.'

'Who we shoot on sight?' says Augustus, shuffling to try and find a comfortable spot on the mower's grass box.

'He needs to get here first. The emperor wants the ring.'

'Wouldn't we be better placed inside the house?'

'Too risky. The crystal keeper is sensitive. I don't want any alarms. Anyway, finding the crystal isn't the end of their journey. We still have the well if this option fails.'

'You think that's where the gangster will go?'

Hector sucks in a deep breath. 'Who knows? Hopefully it will all end here. I'll get back on the street and keep watch from the front. You two stay put.'

*

Conscious of the humans still heading for the back door, Hector creeps behind the shed, makes swift, light work of the garden wall and lands with a gentle thud in the alley. He walks to the street, crosses the road and positions himself in the tobacconist's doorway opposite the bookshop, resting his back on the bricks behind him. He reaches into his coat pocket to retrieve the cigarettes and matches, strikes once, lights the shag and blows smoke into the night air.

A black cat races down the opposite side of the street.

He looks in the direction it came from, expecting to see a pursuer, maybe another cat or a human, but there's no one, just a line of parked cars. He draws again on the cigarette and thinks about his meeting with the captain, confusion clouding his head. Choosing the wrong side now would be foolish. It's okay saying his first duty is to the ecclesia, but who's in charge matters. The gangster is expendable, but the princess obviously cares about her champion. Being the Jinga who signs his death warrant risks Livia's fury, but, on the other hand, he can't fail the emperor. He closes his eyes briefly and then opens them again. The adrenochrome still soothes his system, but he can't relax. He needs to plot his next actions very carefully.

LVIII

Fats eases down in the driver's seat of a Ford Escort and grins at the firefly glow of the Jinga's fag, showing him out in the shop doorway. A schoolboy error in the world of surveillance, but he forgives his adversary's non-human ignorance. Padding these streets undetected is an art form that needs to be mastered, and there are some things that have to be learnt. Like, never stand in the street like a cliché spook. Too risky and too cold. Much better to break into a car, and a piece of piss with old Fords like this one. They might as well leave the key blue-tacked to the roof. And no one ever looks in parked cars. They just sit there, especially in the dark.

He crouches lower and looks through the windscreen at the cloudless night sky. A full moon with stars scattering out in all directions. The sort of night when, as a kid, he would lie flat on his back staring upwards, swamped by the vista of endless galaxies. But now, since he's seen things from above, through the window of the princess's atrium, the magic and mystery has been diluted. They're no longer dreamy portals to another world but just another jumping place for creatures to play games.

He touches the ring – his tracker. *Why aren't the Jinga coming to get me?* They seem to have given up the chase, which suggests they know where he'll emerge. He's disposable, shit on their shoes. That much has been obvious from the start, but he thought the thrill of the hunt would take longer to evaporate. The champion and his girl have been exposed, which means the ring is back in play for them. He's expected to deliver it, explain what's happened and then they kiss and disappear, leaving him out in the open. Something's not right, though. They're inside the bookshop, but the Jinga are waiting. And the only thing they can be waiting for is him. Then why not come over and get him? It doesn't make sense.

He shrugs and runs through his options again. It doesn't take long. Get the crystals and take the vacant escape plan is his only route now. That much is obvious, but it doesn't need to happen here. He can wait. Let the champion and his girl do their gathering and then trail them. The Jinga want the ring, which is probably the only thing keeping him in the game. The only possible flaw is upsetting the princess, but he'll have to take that risk. Anyway, him getting caught wouldn't be smart if she wants to beat her daddy.

That's it, then. If they're not tracking him, he'll wait. Turn down the chance to be the cavalry. He feels like Custer and everyone knows what happened to him. He'll become a street hound. Reverse the chase. Track them in his own way.

Peter Gabriel's 'Games Without Frontiers' starts up in his head.

LIX

Rico jams a piece of tree branch in the rotting frame and levers once, twice, crunching the window open, splinters of wood flaking to the patio slabs below. 'I can't believe how easy that was.'

Mary looks anxiously at the bookshop, expecting a light to come on, but everything stays silent. 'It must be empty. I hope this is the right place.'

'Let's get in,' he says, hauling himself through, dropping to the floor and offering her his hand. She waves it away, grabs the ledge and pulls herself inside.

They take in the room.

A dimly lit Tiffany lamp hangs from the ceiling, casting long shadows into every corner. On the far wall, there's a rusty bicycle secured with two brackets; underneath this sits an enormous, studded oak chest; on the next wall, a rack rammed with coats of all shapes, sizes and colours.

'What's that smell?' asks Rico.

'Dirt,' says Mary, wrinkling her nose. 'This place

hasn't been occupied for years. The crystal can't be here.'

He looks back at the window and then round the room again. 'Come on,' he says, taking her hand.

They walk towards a doorway, the low-wattage Tiffany light their only guide. Ahead of them, a hallway, its walls lined with framed pictures, mixed faces – young, old, men, women, children – staring into semi-darkness. Mary feels the floor texture change from grubby tiles to sticky carpet and thanks God she's not wearing her sandals and dress. The last thing her skin needs is being exposed to whatever crawls these rooms. She prickles at the thought of blood-sucking fleas, stops, pulls Rico to a standstill. 'Can you hear that?'

A hiss, and then what sounds like a whirring fan.

'Central heating boiler?' suggests Rico.

Laughter rings through the house. Another hiss, and then a whoosh from behind a closed door in front of them, yellow and blue light flickering through the gaps in its frame. 'Don't be afraid,' whispers a man's voice. 'You're safe.'

Mary lets go of Rico's hand and strides across the carpet.

'Wait,' Rico shouts, catching up with her as she puts a hand on the handle. 'The room's on fire. You opening that door means—'

'We can't just stand here. The voice said it was safe.'

'Maybe it's a trap. The Jinga—'

'I don't think they want to burn us alive.'

She presses the handle and throws open the door.

LX

Fats hears the whoosh from the bookshop.

He looks at the Jinga, expecting him to run towards the house, but there's no movement apart from fag glow as the Jinga takes another draw. The street stays quiet, undisturbed, and Fats settles back behind the steering wheel of the Ford. He wonders what's happening and guesses finding the third crystal and the whoosh are linked. Hoop man doesn't seem worried, which means everything is as expected. Maybe the champion and his girl have found what they're looking for. He should get ready to move. Not yet though. Warmth and protection from the Escort is what he needs right now.

He touches the ring again.

They must have stopped tracking him. He hopes so because, if not, he's a sitting duck perched yards away from his hunters. Maybe they know where he is and that's adding to the thrill of the game. He wouldn't put anything past that psycho albino. Setting him up to return the ring would add a bit of spice. They're probably all watching now, having a good laugh at his expense. 'Fuck you,' he says to the dashboard. He laughs, takes in a deep breath, and another. 'Calm down, dickhead,' he mutters. 'Get that paranoia under control.'

He puts his hand in the pocket of his donkey jacket and finds his pack of fags. How he could do with a hit of nicotine, or even a slug of Pernod, but that would be dumb. He looks again at the glow in the shop doorway. An image of Jean drops into his head. She'd have been pleased at his strategy here, smart thinking, keeping his sensible brain in place. She always said his urges would be the death of him. Right, as it turned out, but living on his wits had given him a life at a time when his starting options were limited. He grins at the thought of her finding the pile of ash in the swimming baths, trying to work out who's torched her stash. At least she couldn't blame him. Being dead is the best alibi he's ever had.

'Stay cool, Fats,' he whispers, taking his hand from the coat and settling again in the driver's seat. 'Everything will fall into place, if you wait.'

LXI

The atrium empties and the gods rest again.

Livia sits on her platinum throne, speculating which of them will go first. Her briefing over, all of their questions asked, the time has come for them to draw conclusions – to offer wisdom and advice. But it's never that straightforward. Points to prove; scores to settle. Her bet is on Timus breaking the silence, but maybe not. All of them like to have their say, apart from Darius, who keeps counsel, ready to spread the word swiftly throughout the empire.

Phillippa strokes the head of each goshawk, the birds twisting their necks to stare at her with expectation. She reaches into a leather bag on her lap and lifts out a wriggling mouse, which she swings by its tail and feeds to the first goshawk before dipping into the bag again, fetching out a second rodent and feeding the other bird. Both goshawks swallow in gulping stages and Phillippa kisses their beaks. 'The emperor stays on his quest while the game continues?' she says, meeting Livia's eyes.

'I rule in his absence, Phillippa.'

Timus grunts and rubs his pot belly.

'Indigestion?' says Athos, making Phillippa and Livia smile.

'Not at all. But I'm wondering if this game has a purpose.'

'Perhaps you need to raise that with the emperor,' says Livia.

'I thought you ruled in his absence.'

'Are you being deliberately obtuse?'

'Timus,' says Phillippa, smiling and looking at him, 'you know full well, Octavius likes his games. And this one is about soulmates, which interests me, given the emperor's history.'

Livia takes a sip of her wine. She's been waiting for this subject to rear its head. 'History?'

'Well, we all know what happened to Helena, and then there's Octavius's view on human soulmates. Or is that something you think unconnected?'

'It's obviously so,' says Timus. 'The emperor chases your champion because he runs with a soulmate.'

'And that relates to my mother in what way?'

'Octavius's love for his own human—'

'Careful, Timus,' says Livia, leaning forward on her throne.

'All I'm saying is the emperor loved her like a soulmate, despite his views on the subject.'

'It has to have a bearing,' says Phillippa.

Livia sits back, tries to relax the tension in her body. 'You're saying Octavius's motivation is to break the bond between the humans. But why do that, if his love for my mother shows him the power of soulmates? That doesn't make sense.'

'Why do you think Octavius has such strong views on soulmates?' says Timus.

'Enlighten me.'

'Because he knows he can't have one, and if he can't have—'

Athos claps his hands. 'Enough said. Perhaps another break, Princess.'

Livia stares at him, not saying a word.

'Princess,' says Athos, desperation in his voice, 'let's gather our thoughts before continuing.'

'No. There's something else before we break.'

Athos goes to reply, but she puts up her hand to silence him. 'It's about the monk.'

They all look at the vacant chaise longue.

'I've found out about the brothers.'

'Oh, that,' says Phillippa.

'You knew?'

'Of course. But the emperor swore us to secrecy.'

'So, I've been treated like a child.'

'More protected,' says Athos.

'The monk has behaved like my only kin.'

'Understandable,' says Phillippa. 'He needs your favour.'

'And his role in my mother's fate?'

'He had no role. The brothers were punished.'

'That's not how they see things. I need to question him, even though he's an ecclesia member.'

'Do what you want,' says Timus. 'I never understood why the emperor promoted him in the first place.'

Livia looks at the rest of the gods and they nod in agreement. 'That easy. I wonder if you'd feel the same if it was a god under suspicion.'

'No god would behave in such a way,' says Phillippa.

Athos smiles and looks at the glass floor.

The gong strikes one more time.

LXII

Mary takes a step backwards and puts her hand over her mouth.

'Jesus,' says Rico, staring into the room.

In front of them, on a wooden office chair, sits a man, barefoot and wearing a string vest and tracksuit bottoms. Flames consume his outline from head to foot, his hair strands standing up like individual sparklers, jets of fire shooting out of his fingers and toes. 'Don't be alarmed,' he says.

'Get some water,' screams Mary. 'There must be a bucket in the kitchen.'

Rico turns but stops when the man stands and shouts, 'I'm okay.'

He walks towards them, his arms outstretched.

'Who are you?' says Mary, feeling a heat bath from his body.

'The fireman,' he says, holding a hand to the side of his mouth and glancing furtively round the room, creating a conspiratorial whisper. 'I have your crystal.'

He laughs and prances round them, screaming, 'You're here. You're here,' but comes to a stop when he sees horrified looks on their faces. 'I'll turn it down,' he says, clapping his hands. The flames diminish to an ember glow. He reaches out and pulls them close.

Mary winces at his hug, expecting to be scolded, but all she feels is a warm touch, barely penetrating her hoodie. 'You frightened the life out of me.'

'Sorry,' he says, stepping back. 'I forget my appearance might alarm others.' He points at two seats next to the one he's vacated. 'I've made tea,' he says, standing next to a table laden with a fully laid-up service: China cups, saucers, milk jug, sugar bowl and a teapot; next to this a cake stand with an assortment of choux buns, chocolate eclairs and Victoria sponge slices. He sits back in his chair, a halo surrounding his body. 'Shall I pour?'

Rico looks at Mary and they nod, taking their seats. 'Does it hurt?' she says, gesturing towards the man's scorched lips.

'Not at all,' he says, splashing milk and tea into three cups. 'Help yourself to sugar and cakes.'

LXIII

Bernard rushes along the link corridor from the Jinga starship, into the safety of the princess's top-of-the-world atrium. His journey back through wormholes and connecting portals has left him nauseous, a price he pays for his human genes. The emperor's gift of immortality has not changed his physical DNA one iota, which means his body reacts to every bump through and across chasms of distance and time, a reminder of his existential fragility. At least he's in solid form, unlike his smoke brothers.

The Jinga captain's words replay in his mind. A strong hint to make Livia aware of concerns for the emperor's welfare, but leaving Bernard exposed as messenger. And the emperor's behaviour: a black hole obsession, placing the whole crew in jeopardy; the card game predominating his thoughts after so many years. The mystery is why. Maybe the Jinga is right. Time away in the cosmos wilderness and the battles with Livia have tilted Octavius into madness.

It could be an opportunity, a shift of power. If so, he needs to be on the right side of change. He smiles at the thought and quickens his pace but then slows again when he spots the princess's eight-foot albino standing at the end of the walkway.

'Good evening,' says Sebastian, as Bernard reaches him.

'A welcoming committee. To what do I owe the pleasure?'

'Her Highness would like a word.'

'I was planning—'

'Straight away,' says Sebastian, taking Bernard's arm, his pink eyes drilling into the monk's face.

'There's no need—'

'Walk,' snarls Sebastian.

*

In a basement cell, Bernard sucks a deep breath, which he regrets when a pungency of stale sweat fills his nostrils. He sniffs the cassock's armpits, expecting himself to be the source after the day he's had, but there's nothing. He looks round the room. White walls, floor, ceiling; no windows; a table, the hardback chair he's sitting on and another chair in front of him. Artificial light glares and reflects, making it difficult to keep his eyes open. He dreads what next. The signs aren't good. The albino dumping him here with no explanation, in what looks like a holding pen, means danger. What he's trying to work out is why and how much he should be worried.

He spools through his memory of the conversation with the Jinga. The two things must be connected. Perhaps the emperor set a trap. Then why is he here, awaiting the princess? None of it makes sense. His answers to the captain were ambiguous, giving him time to think.

The door opens and he jumps to his feet.

Sebastian enters, stands to one side, and Livia walks in behind him.

'Your Highness,' says Bernard. 'What—'

His words are cut short as Sebastian marches over and pushes him back into the chair. Livia positions herself in front of him. 'Just answer my questions. Why have you been meeting with Octavius?'

'But—' A punch lands on the side of his head, making him recoil – confusion, shock, pain filling his brain. He glares at the albino, but all he gets back are dead eyes, and then looks at Livia, who leans with her back against the wall. 'I thought I was family.'

'Tell me why, or he'll punch you again.'

'He wanted to know about the card game, tries to make sense of what happened.'

Livia looks at Sebastian, who pulls out the second chair. She takes a seat directly opposite the monk and puts her hands on the table. 'Talk.'

'I don't understand.'

'Octavius's summons is about more than your presence at the game.'

'He wanted my recollection.'

'But why you? There were lots of people watching. And I thought the reason for my mother's fate was clear.'

'The emperor's guilt weighs on him. He seeks another explanation.'

'Like the smoke humans?'

The words hit him like bullets. He hesitates, sees Livia look at Sebastian, who steps closer to the table.

'That was a question,' she spits, leaning forwards.

'Everyone was sworn to secrecy.'

'Why hide their involvement? They're just humans, and why let them continue to exist?'

Bernard looks into her eyes and then at the albino. He drops his head. 'They're the empress's brothers.'

'Which means they're my family?'

'I couldn't tell you before because—'

'You let me believe you were my only blood, my trusted advisor.'

'The emperor—'

'Have you been spying on me all along?'

'No—'

'Tell me about the card game.'

'What?'

Another punch hits him in the face.

'The card game. I want to know about your involvement in my mother's fate.'

'I'm a member of the ecclesia,' splutters Bernard, holding his nose, pain screaming at the back of his eyes. 'You can't beat me like this.'

'You think they care about you? Tell me what happened.'

'Your father lost.'

'Then why punish the smoke humans?'

'Easier than blaming himself. It drives him mad, makes him act irrationally, and I've heard he talks strategy with his harpy.'

'You doubt the emperor's state of mind?'

'I'm not alone,' says Bernard, wiping his hands down the arms of the cassock. 'Even the Jinga are worried. The captain asked me to speak to you. Your father's grief overwhelms him.'

'A Jinga captain said that?'

'Before I left the emperor's starship. I didn't tell you about my half-brothers because of the embargo, but no one had any involvement in what happened to Helena apart from Octavius, and it tears him to pieces.'

Livia turns to Sebastian. 'Can we speak to this captain without raising suspicions?'

Sebastian shakes his head. 'That won't be easy. He's your father's bodyguard.'

'Find a way. There's a lieutenant chasing the

gangster. Pay him a visit. Plant a seed of doubt. This could be useful.' She glares at Bernard again. 'How could you deny your family, let them suffer?'

'I had no choice,' he stutters. 'I was coming to tell you.'

'Forgive me if I don't trust what you say. You'll remain here until we've spoken to the Jinga.'

'Your father will know.'

'That depends on how we ask.'

*

Bernard sits alone in the white room, staring at the wall, pondering how quickly the safety and certainty of his world crashes down – like a centuries old tree caught off-guard by a gale blowing in precisely the right direction. A human out of place. It was astonishing he'd rooted for so long. He knew the origin of his demise, but he didn't understand why. For aeons the smoke humans had lived with their lie. Why choose now to bleed the truth, forcing him to reveal the Jinga's worries? He curses under his breath. He wanted time to think, to work out the right strategy, but he'd had to blurt it out to save his skin.

He pours himself a tumbler of water from the glass jug Sebastian dumped on the table. The bastard albino had thumped him twice and then left him to stew in his own juices. That'll not be forgotten if he can find a way back. Perhaps all is not lost. The kindness of the water tells him Livia still has some compassion for him. He is, after all, family.

A noise in the corridor behind the door speeds his pulse.

Someone walking by.

He takes a gulp of water and smiles. He has one trick up his sleeve. Perhaps it's time to reveal the full truth of the card game, bring out his ace in the pack.

Bring to centre stage the god who helped Wrath to victory.

LXIV

Livia re-enters the atrium as cheers ring out from the audience.

She follows everyone's gaze to the glass ceiling and the sight of copious yellow, blue and red asteroids orbiting a sun, rolling along a gravitational pull like a bag of marbles. Suddenly, a puff of explosion in the galaxy as a star dies, sending streaks of fizzing light across the cosmos. Another cheer from the crowd, closely followed by a screech from the goshawks, Phillippa and Timus standing side by side on stage, their eyes fixed on the vista.

Athos puts up his hand in greeting, pushes through the throng and comes to her side. 'You've spoken to the monk?'

She picks up a goblet of wine from a table next to her and takes a sip. 'He's answering my questions.'

'But are they questions you should be asking?'

'I need to know, Athos. Surely, that's something you understand.'

'The emperor lost a card game. One he should not have been playing.'

'You sound worried.'

'About you. Nothing else.'

He takes her hand and strokes the palm with his forefinger.

She feels the warmth from his touch and looks into his eyes. 'A bold move.'

'Instinctive. And long overdue. You can't be surprised.'

'Octavius would never let me reciprocate.'

'I live in hope, and I notice you've not pulled away.'

'Now is not the right time.'

'Then I'll wait with the patience of a god and a warrior.'

She laughs. 'I'm not sure it's your greatest virtue.'

He bows. 'For you, I'll make an exception.'

LXV

Darkness interrupted by street lights casts shadows across the road and parked cars – everything quiet after the whoosh – and Hector sucks a last drag of his cigarette before throwing it to the ground and crushing the nub end into the pavement with the heel of his boot. He takes in the drizzle-stained tarmac and the bookshop in front of him, hoping the fireman has completed his histrionics. Every Jinga knows the drama queen crystal keeper who struggles to keep control of his emotions and decisions. It's how he got into a mess in the first place.

A meow shifts Hector's gaze, and his eyes fall on the spooked black cat from earlier, now tilting its head and watching him from the opposite pavement. He smiles at the cat's eyes, the left one askew, lower than the right, giving the moggy a cockeyed stare – an extra layer of cuteness. *Humans and their animals*, he thinks. The only species he's ever come across that can be so cruel to other creatures but also so kind and compassionate.

The cat pads across the road, reaches Hector, purring and weaving in-between his legs. 'Who owns you?' says Hector, crouching and scratching the cat's head.

'The princess,' says the cat.

Hector stands and steps backwards. 'I recognise—'

'Sebastian. And we've met before. I have a message.'

Hector looks nervously towards the bookshop and up the street. 'The emperor would not like—'

'Maybe you need to think about the princess and what she'd like.'

'What do you mean?'

'She's aware of her father's frailty. Does it not bother you?'

'I'm told the emperor is in good health,' stammers Hector.

'I hear the truth in your voice. Do you really want to be in the princess's bad books if that's not the case?'

And with that the cat struts away, leaving Hector fumbling in his pocket for cigarettes.

LXVI

Fats knows something weird has just happened, but he's not sure exactly what.

If he didn't know any better, he'd swear a cat just spoke to the Jinga, spooked him and then padded away with his tail in the air. In his old life, he'd be taking a break from the wacky baccy now. Getting the occasional munchies is one thing, but hallucinating talking cats is something else. But that's exactly what he saw and, judging by the way the Jinga urgently puffs on his fag, whatever the cat said hit the mark.

He looks at the bookshop.

It's still in darkness.

What's taking the champion and his girl so long?

The back of his left hand itches and he scratches away. He should move. Staying in one spot is pushing his luck, even if they've stopped tracking him. He considers this for a second and realises he has nowhere to go. Waiting for the crystals and the well is his only option. That's not good. His whole life has been about boltholes of escape, and now, for the first time, he finds himself in a run-for-it cul-de-sac.

He looks again at the Jinga.

A talking cat.

For fuck's sake.

LXVII

The fireman sips his tea and studies the couple. He can't believe they're here after all these years. The princess said they'd come, but that was decades ago, and he'd almost given up hope. Mary and Rico. Nice names, and the way they look at each other reminds him of his wife, his children, his family.

'You've been expecting us?' says Mary.

'Forever,' he replies. 'How are the cakes?'

Cream drips through Rico's lips as he takes a bite of a choux bun. 'Fantastic,' he splutters, spraying flakes of pastry.

Mary glares at him and hands over a napkin.

'Eat what you want,' says the fireman. 'Enjoy yourselves. My home is here for you to savour.'

'Actually,' says Rico, dabbing his chin, 'we could do with moving on. We're in a sort of race.'

'So quickly?' says the fireman, leaping from his seat and sending sparks from his fingertips. 'You've only just arrived.'

Rico places his half-eaten cake back on the table. 'Perhaps a little longer. Do you live here alone?'

The fireman sits back down and crosses his legs. He grabs his foot to try and stop it twitching and runs his sparking fingers through his ember-laden hair. 'Ever since my wife and children… but I mustn't talk about that. It upsets me.'

'We don't want to do that.'

'No,' says the fireman, and then he bursts into tears.

Mary puts her cup and saucer on the table and pulls him to her, letting him sob into her hoodie. 'It's okay,' she whispers.

He lifts his head. 'It is now you're here. The princess will return my family.'

'You mean they're dead.'

'Moved on. But I'll see them soon.' He waves his hand and sniffs. 'Silly me and my experiments.'

Mary looks at Rico and then, for the first time, round the room. Shiny marble tiles cover the far wall and ceiling, and, on another wall, what looks like a list of chemical elements painted in ancient script. Apart from the three chairs and table with the afternoon tea, the only other items of furniture are work benches loaded with vials, microscopes and Bunsen burners, and a floor-to-ceiling bookcase laden with dusty volumes that look like they've never been read. 'You're a scientist.'

'Of sorts. The princess lets me dabble.'

'But something went wrong?'

'All these chemicals,' says the fireman, uncrossing his legs and waving his hand. 'They confuse me.'

'You blew up the house,' says Rico.

Tremors consume the fireman's body; his halo glows brighter. 'I didn't mean...' he screams, jumping up again. 'It was an accident. I told them, and the princess. I didn't mean...' He strides round the chairs, heat spots shifting from yellow, to blue, to white... 'I can't control...'

'Sit down,' shouts Mary, standing up and taking his arm, bringing him to a standstill. 'You're getting into a state.'

The fireman looks startled. He registers her expression and retakes his seat.

'Now, tell us what happened,' she says, gently squeezing his hand.

'An explosion. I mixed the wrong gasses.'

'But you got out?'

'We all died. My family were asleep upstairs; stood no chance.'

Rico gives him an incredulous look. 'This house burnt down?'

'I had to have somewhere to wait. The princess pulled me back from limbo, rebuilt my home, gave me this job and her promise.' The glow around his body flickers. 'Now you're here, I can rejoin them.'

'You're still doing experiments?'

'That's my job. The princess needs to know how things work. But she's promised me my freedom. As soon as you take the crystal.' He smiles at them. 'I've just realised the quicker you leave, the sooner I'll see them. Follow me. It's time for you to go.'

*

They pace behind him down the hall, past the line of pictures with lifeless eyes staring out, the fireman's full-body halo guiding their path. They reach the room where they entered the bookshop, the rusty bicycle frame still hanging on the wall over the oak chest.

'Did you have to force the window?' says the fireman, glaring at Rico.

'No choice.'

'You could have knocked.'

'We never thought of that.'

Mary looks at the rammed coatrack, anonymous when they climbed in but now triggering a sadness as she remembers the fates of the wearers.

'They'll be back soon,' says the fireman, smiling at her. 'We just need to get you sorted.' He kneels in front of the chest, flips the clasps open to raise the lid and pulls the third labradorite crystal into the room: a triangle of amber translucence glowing up at them from the slate tile floor.

Mary kneels and strokes it. 'The same size as the others.' She reaches into Rico's backpack and fetches the square block dropped overboard by the chug captain and then unzips her bag and retrieves the football piece from the Roman soldier. She sits them in a line, the fireman's triangle in the centre. 'They're beautiful.'

'I'm told the sun makes their veins throb,' says the fireman.

'They come alive,' she says, looking up at him. 'What will you do now?'

'The princess will save me.'

'And you'll see your family?'

The fireman nods.

She sees tears being squeezed back in his eyes. Those coats, everything kept the same, waiting for his wife and children to return. He's like her father, trying to do the best he can but getting it badly wrong. She reaches out and hugs him. 'You mustn't blame yourself. It was an accident.'

'I've served my penance.'

'I hope you're reunited quickly.'

Rico pushes the crystals back into the two backpacks, loading the round and square one into his and the triangle one into Mary's. 'We need to go.'

'I'll open the backdoor,' says the fireman. 'Be careful. They're out there, watching you.'

'We suspected as much, but we've no choice but to press on.'

'Good luck,' says the fireman, taking a key from his pocket.

He opens the door and watches them disappear down the alley, smiling as they grab each other's hands. 'I'm waiting, Princess,' he mutters. 'It's time to keep your promise.'

LXVIII

Fats watches the champion and his girl emerge into the street. They stand still for a second and study a map, looking as though they're getting their bearings. He notes the Jinga in the doorway opposite step back into the shadows. So, the pursuit is all about him and the ring, but why isn't he being tracked? Nothing in this crazy, fucked-up world adds up.

He eases the car door open and slides onto the pavement. Keeping low, he peeps over the wing and waits.

The couple look up the street, the champion pointing towards the Escort. For a moment, Fats thinks he's been seen as they walk towards him, but they cross over and head away in the direction of the main road. The Jinga strides across the pavement and back up the alley. Why isn't he following? The only conclusion Fats can reach is that he already knows where they're going. It's the only thing that makes sense. Well, that makes his job easier. He needs to keep the crystals in sight. He'll give them the ring and then…

'The princess is watching you, buddy.'

He turns at the sound of the familiar voice.

A black cat sits in front of him, licking its front paw and cleaning its face. 'You've not returned the ring,' purrs the cat.

'I'm trying, but the crazies are keeping a close watch. How come these guys aren't tracking me?'

'The emperor has decided to catch everyone the old-fashioned way.'

'He must be confident.'

'All you have to do is get the ring to the champion.'

Fats looks up the street and then back at the alleyway and bookshop. 'They're nearly out of sight.'

'Then you'd better go. The Jinga have no need to track the couple. They know their destination.'

'It's me they're after.'

'Only because you have the ring. The quicker you make your delivery, the safer you'll be, and the princess will reward you.'

And with that the cat sashays away.

'Screw that,' whispers Fats. 'I'll look after myself.'

LXIX

Livia settles on her throne and waits for the gods to retake their positions. She ponders her next move, weighs up the pros and cons of what she's about to do and decides there's no other way. It must be brought out in the open, even if it triggers a reaction from Octavius. At some point it has to come to a head. She nods at muscle man, who strikes to recommence the meeting and an evacuation of the auditorium guests.

'Is the monk being helpful?' says Timus.

Livia sighs. 'He worries about Octavius's health, says the Jinga have concerns.'

'The Jinga? They wouldn't dare. Who?'

'A captain,' says Livia, pausing to let the status of the information source sink home. 'He claims the loss of my mother swamps the emperor with grief.'

'Like we said earlier,' says Phillippa, tugging one of her goshawks back into position on her shoulder, 'he's lost his soulmate.'

'What exactly is this Jinga captain meant to have said?' says Athos.

Timus waves his hand dismissively. 'It's all nonsense and comes from a monk human in fear of his life.'

Livia stands and walks over to the plasma pool, nonchalantly dipping her hand, breaking the surface, causing a flow of ripples. 'He's my mother's half-brother, Timus. And Octavius appointed him to the ecclesia.'

'Tell the emperor what he claims, and his life will be worthless.'

'But what if it's true?' says Phillippa. 'Should we not at least talk to the Jinga?'

'I don't see how,' says Timus. 'Not without the emperor finding out.'

'We could send the messenger of gods,' says Livia. 'He's swift enough to evade attention.'

All eyes fall on Darius.

LXX

The captain slouches on his carbon fibre pouffe, having left Octavius consumed with his harpy and bemoaning the fate of the empress. He's grateful for the chance to gather his thoughts and hopes Hector is making progress, playing a game the emperor seems less and less concerned about. Switching off the tracker has made things complicated.

He kicks off his caligae, wriggles his toes, takes a sip of adrenochrome and closes his eyes, savouring the nectar in his mouth before he swallows. What the hell is the emperor playing at? He reminds himself of who he is. A Jinga captain who needs to do his duty as always. What happens next is uppermost in his mind. How to deal with the emperor's madness? He knows the monk is a coward, but a greedy one who might spot a strategic advantage. That would be the best way of bringing things to the attention of the ecclesia. The only way if he wants to keep breathing.

'Good evening, Captain.'

His eyes flash open. Sitting in the corner of the room, hovering just underneath the ceiling, is the winged god, Darius. 'Your Highness,' he says, sitting up and nearly spilling his drink. 'I didn't hear—'

'I need to speak with you,' says Darius, cutting across the captain's words. 'Not even Octavius can know.'

'But what—'

'You've raised concern about the emperor's health. Tell me and leave nothing out.'

'It's not for me to—'

'It's too late for subtleties and duty. Your only hope is serving the ecclesia and praying the princess will show mercy. Now say, and quickly.' Darius's choirboy eyes twinkle as he stamps out his last sentence, his winged feet fluttering to hold position.

The captain feels the warning in the god's icy stare, telling him he has no choice. He drops his head for a second and then looks up again. 'The emperor grieves Helena. The only thing holding his attention is the harpy he keeps for company.'

'His harpy?'

'He talks to it day and night, asks its advice on how to get the empress back.'

Darius lifts an eyebrow. 'He means to challenge Wrath?'

'It appears so.'

'But that would be a declaration of war.'

'That's my concern, Your Highness. I've been contemplating what to do. It gives me no pleasure to report on the emperor.'

'I understand your dilemma. Is Octavius still committed to this game?'

'Less and less. His thoughts are consumed by the empress.'

'Say nothing. I'll report to the ecclesia and the princess. You've done well. I'm sure your loyalty will be rewarded.'

And with that the god disappears, leaving the captain to stare at an empty space. He downs what remains in his vial of adrenochrome and walks over to the cabinet for a refill.

LXXI

Octavius looks at the plasma pool and wonders if it's worth trying again to negotiate with Wrath. He glances out of the window at a new, unexplored galaxy. Anchoring on the edge of the unknown used to excite him, satisfy his yearning to bring new species into his empire, but an adrenalin rush alludes him for now. Millions and millions of galaxies, but all he can think about is one planet and one human. Behind him, sat on her perch, he hears Penelope cleaning her wings. He knows there's nothing more she can say; her advice is clear. 'She loves you. Get her back.' If only it were that easy. Wrath holds all the cards, and the only way to rescue Helena is by force, and that means triggering chaos across the afterlife, with all gods forced to take sides. He wishes he could talk to Livia, agree a father–daughter strategy, but that's impossible, especially during the middle of this ridiculous game.

'Captain,' he calls.

'Your Highness,' says the captain, walking onto the starship deck.

'You are rested?'

'I am.'

Octavius meets his eyes. 'Update me. Where are the humans?'

'The champion and his girl are in sight, but there's no sign of the gangster.'

'I'm assuming the Jinga are waiting at the well.'

'They're heading that way.'

'Then the gangster will appear at some point. Is there anything else?'

'Nothing, sir.'

'Are you sure? You look uncomfortable. Has something happened?'

'It's just...'

'Spit it out, man. You're a Jinga. This isn't like you.'

'The monk... the princess questions the monk.'

Octavius strides over and grabs the captain's throat. 'And why is she doing that?'

'I don't know, sir.'

'You don't know. I thought your spies had infiltrated every level. Has this been approved by the ecclesia?'

'I be-believe so, sir.'

'And now you're stuttering,' spits the emperor, leaning closer into the captain's face. 'What are you not telling me?'

The captain tries to pull back, but the emperor tightens his grip. 'The princess has found out about the smoke humans, Your Highness. She wants the monk to explain and tell her about the card game.'

'Why is that so hard to say?'

'I… I don't know. You've been…'

'I've told you before about presuming to know my thoughts.'

'Yes, sir.'

'Are you doubting me?'

'Your Majesty?'

'I need to know you're still loyal. Perhaps it's time you went back to the ranks, or we could revisit the black hole.'

'Your Highness, I would never—'

Octavius pushes him away. 'Find out what the monk has told Livia. Now go.'

'Yes, sir,' says the captain, saluting and clicking his heels together before marching out of the room.

The emperor walks over to the birdcage and rattles his fingers across the bars. 'An ecclesia approved interrogation of an ecclesia member.'

Penelope blinks and hops over to him, letting him scratch her neck. 'He is a human.'

'Even so, Livia risks a lot. She must know about the brothers, and I'm guessing she feels betrayed. Bernard has played the loyal uncle so well over the years.'

'She misses her mother.'

'Something we share.'

'Maybe it's time you talked to her.'

'Perhaps, and it's also necessary to talk to the ecclesia, remind them of their place. First, though, we must settle this game. Make sure there are no distractions.'

He turns again towards the plasma pool.

LXXII

Hector reaches the bin and stares up at a cloud-free night sky. As he watches, more and more stars flicker into view, as though someone sprinkles them for his entertainment. Up there, somewhere, is the emperor's starship and the princess's top-of-the-world atrium. Father and daughter embroiled in a game that means life and death for its participants. He's one of those pawns, having to decide who to back, running the risk of being on the wrong side. The captain has made up his mind, and the cat's warning has hit home. How frail is the emperor? He's certainly behaving out of character, but that doesn't mean the princess will prevail. He needs to think it through, plan his moves carefully. For now, he has his orders.

He clambers up on the bin lid, jumps to the top of the wall and scrambles down the other side to land on the lawn.

The shed door opens as he strides across the grass.

His fellow Jinga step out into the night. 'Is all well, sir?' says Augustus.

'The champion and his girl have left. I'm assuming they have the crystals.'

'And the gangster?'

'No sign, but we know where they're heading.'

'Shouldn't we search for him here?'

'Questioning my order again, Augustus. This is becoming a habit.'

'I'm just checking, sir.'

'We're heading for the well. Let's go.'

'What about the fireman?' asks Anthony.

'He's nothing to do with us,' replies Hector, striding back across the grass.

The two Jinga warriors look at each other and then follow.

LXXIII

Octavius rests his head against the cushion behind him and closes his eyes.

Before he does anything else, he has to rest.

He tries to recall the last time he slept, but being a god excuses him of the need. Even so, he misses his nights of perfect cave dreams, the times of being a boy again, everything tickling his spirit of adventure. And then he fell in love, memories of days spent holding Helena, embracing her for all eternity, wishing time would stand still. All of this kept him company in the reverie hours, but now only guilt and regret await, and a desperate longing to put everything right.

He feels slumber wash over him.

A mist on the horizon lifts; ripples of air drift his way; and he knows she's there. Long, shiny black hair, chocolate-brown eyes. She floats towards him across a milky ocean, sitting cross-legged on a lotus flower. 'Save me,' she calls, holding out her arms.

Octavius's eyes flash open.

He looks at the birdcage.

Penelope stares at him through the bars. 'You need to get her back,' she whispers.

LXXIV

Pandemonium breaks out in the atrium: the gods talking over each other; Phillippa's goshawks screeching and jumping up and down on her shoulders.

'Silence,' calls Livia. 'Let Darius finish his report.'

The gong sounds. Everyone hushes and faces the striker, Athos, who has extended his height to ceiling level. 'For God's sake,' he booms, 'sit down. We're not children.'

With a final grunt and scowl, Timus settles again on his chaise longue. All the other gods follow suit, including Athos, who shrinks back to human size. Phillippa pulls her goshawks' jesses tighter and threatens to hood them if they continue to jump about.

'Darius,' says Livia.

The messenger god smiles, his cherub, freckled face beaming as he takes centre stage once more. He flutters his winged feet to rise above his fellow gods. 'The captain reports concern about the emperor's grief.'

'A Jinga captain has no right,' says Timus.

'You will let Darius complete his report,' snaps Livia.

'It doesn't matter what he says. Octavius can do what he likes, and this captain is a traitor.'

'Continue, Darius.'

'The emperor intends to confront Wrath.'

'But that would mean—'

'War,' says Timus.

'That can't happen,' says Phillippa. 'Octavius must be persuaded.'

'That's why the captain chose to report the emperor,' says Darius. 'He's anguished long and hard over what to do.'

'So,' says Athos, 'the monk was right. Shouldn't we allow him to take his seat?'

'He kept the truth from me about the smoke humans,' says Livia.

'With the best intentions.'

She holds his gaze for a second and then waves towards Sebastian, who is standing at the edge of the auditorium. 'Bring Bernard. We need a full ecclesia to debate our next steps.'

'We should also summon the teller sisters,' says Phillippa.

'Mumbo jumbo,' says Timus. 'We need to speak with the emperor.'

'Would you like to do that, Timus?' says Livia.

'You're the emperor delegate in Octavius's absence.'

'Accusing my father of frailty won't go down well.'

'Neither will discussing him behind his back.'

'We have to do something. Tell the sisters we need a weave.'

'I'll prepare the loom,' says Phillippa.

LXXV

Fats hunches into his donkey jacket to try and find residual warmth, but there's no way of driving the chill from his bones. Ahead of him he sees the sun rising above the misty hillside, but it'll be a while before it delivers any heat. Frosty breath stains the air in front of his face. It's been a long night, trekking through a wood and along dirt tracks on the outskirts of town, trying to keep the champion and his girl in sight. The mossy ground is slippery with dew and he's glad of the Doc Martens, perfect for tramping and keeping him upright.

The route surprises him. He's lived in this town all his life but never ventured into these parts. He doesn't know anyone who has, and he should. This looks like ideal gangster land: miles from anywhere; not a living soul; perfect for a deal or a hit; foolproof for hiding bodies. It can't be real. It must be manufactured as part of the bonkers game he's been dragged into. He shivers and pulls the collar of the donkey jacket up higher. 'Better than being dead,' he tells himself, and carries on walking.

Up ahead, his prey turns a corner and disappears. He speeds up, ready to dodge into the wood if necessary. He sees them again, still on the dirt track. They've stopped. The champion is looking at the map and pointing, but the girl shakes her head. They're disagreeing. Fats leans against a tree, lights a cigarette and grins. From what he saw earlier in the desert, Champ might as well give it up. She's definitely the brains of the operation.

Sure enough, they turn off the track and start to climb the hill into the woods.

Fats blows smoke skywards, spits out a stray sliver of tobacco and follows them.

LXXVI

Rico leads the scramble up the hillside, but he's not convinced they're going the right way. All he sees are trees and there's no discernible landmark that shouts 'to the well', but Mary is positive, feels it in her water that this is the right way. He hates her premonitions and intuitions, but he has to admit there's something inside of her that he can't explain. Anyway, the map is inconclusive, just a track line with X marking the spot, and his only alternative is to carry on walking with a hit and hope. That doesn't seem much better.

'Can you see anything?' shouts Mary into his back.

'Trees. Nothing but trees.'

'Keep going. I know this is right.'

He shifts his backpack, trying to get it more comfortable, feeling the weight of two crystals. Thank God they both have backpacks and Mary carries the third labradorite. Ahead of him he sees a clearing halfway up the hill. He's not hopeful. He doesn't know much about wells, but surely this isn't a likely place to find one. 'There's a glade up ahead,' he calls back, 'but I can't see a well.'

Her scrambling gets louder as she catches up and comes alongside him. 'That must be it,' she says, brushing dirt from her hands.

'Let's get closer,' he says. 'Perhaps the well is hidden. We still don't know what to do with the crystals when we get there.'

'The one thing I've learnt about your princess is her message will arrive.'

A noise of breaking twigs down the hillside makes them both glance back.

'Probably some wild animal,' she says.

'Or the Jinga. They must know we're here. Why aren't they showing themselves?'

'Maybe they're busy with Fats. I wonder how he's getting on.'

'We need to look after ourselves. Come on.'

LXXVII

Fats curses under his breath as he ducks behind a tree. He sneaks a look up the hill. Mary and Rico have turned away again, but the Jinga might have heard that noise and be heading for him through the forest. He flashes a look in all directions. Nothing, but that doesn't mean anything. They probably wouldn't bother chasing him, just take him out from a distance. He thinks about the bloke in the bar. Escaping has probably forfeited his right to be captured and plead his case. They'll take no chances next time. He shrugs. 'Can't keep dodging the bullets forever,' he tells himself. He knows he's had his share of good luck over the years. In his profession, death usually comes without consent. He's learnt to live every moment. And then he remembers the pool and mutters to himself, 'You're already dead, you daft fucker.'

He risks another look round the tree.

They're on the move, heading for what looks like a clearing up ahead. He touches the ring and wonders what the champion and his girl have been told about the change of rules in the game, that the emperor has stopped tracking everyone. He's noticed the camel has gone. Perhaps that was a punishment. Who knows what that twisted albino could think up?

He looks behind him one more time and scrambles after them.

LXXVIII

The captain kneels by his bed and prays. He's not sure who he's praying to. Gods looking out for gods, if such a realm exists. That bit has never been explained, but he's ready to find out. Maybe there's a higher spiritual place for deities who have served well. He hopes it's not Wrath, but so be it. He'll have to grin and bear his destiny.

The rituals have been followed to the letter – bathing in eucalyptus oil to cleanse his physical body; deep meditation to balm his soul; putting on a black death toga to wear into his next existence. He has no regrets, and there are no family to mourn him. He's breathed every breath for the empire. In front of him, stacked in neat piles, are his Jinga uniforms – leather fighting panels, plumed helmets, ceremonial dress, caligae for all occasions – and his medals awarded for many acts of valour over decades of service. He removes the hoop ring from his nose and places it on a pillow. He's done his duty, but the time has come to exit.

He picks up his dagger.

Octavius's question about soulmates comes into his mind. He'd managed to avoid answering the emperor, had been too frightened to venture a view on the subject, but he realises now, right at the end, that he doesn't really have an opinion. It's never come up as an option in his life. It would have been nice to have someone to share this existence with, but, for a dedicated Jinga, that was never going to work. He wishes he could explain his motives to the emperor for raising his concerns with the ecclesia, but that is a futile desire. Octavius will discover the betrayal, and nothing can save him from the fury that will burst from the emperor's gut. Much better he controls the where, when and how. He knows Octavius and his vivid imagination when dreaming up methods of revenge. Suffice to say, there are lots of ways to die, some more unpleasant than others. At least this way he keeps control and retains his dignity.

He slugs back a vial of adrenochrome.

Thinking of nothing, he plunges the dagger into his chest.

LXXIX

Octavius looks round the starship's stainless-steel morgue and shivers. Death and the dead make him uneasy, even though he's a god and the supreme ruler of human afterlife. The evidence of what happens to gods when they die is sparse. Not something the elite have to worry about, blessed as they are with immortality, but for the lesser gods it's an eternal mystery. He supposes there must be another realm, divided into empires, shared out amongst… He doesn't want to think about it. If such a place exists, it suggests a higher form of being, a race of super gods, but, if that's the case, where does it end? Perhaps it loops back on itself for all eternity.

'Ready, Your Majesty?' says Cicero.

Octavius looks down at the gurney.

Cicero pulls back the sheet.

A grimaced face stares up at them.

'He looks as though he died in pain,' says Octavius, putting his hands behind his back and studying the Jinga.

'Possibly. There were easier ways for him to exit.'

'Not for a Jinga, Cicero. This was his only means. He'll be hoping for absolution in the next realm.'

'Your Majesty?'

'For his treachery. He betrayed me. I'm yet to find out how, but that's why he chose the coward's route.'

'He served you for many years and—'

'A traitor in the end. I could bring him back to face his punishment.'

'But that would be—'

'Against the natural order and the ethics of our realm. But I'm the emperor, Cicero. Is it not my prerogative to…' Octavius catches himself, reaches down and touches the captain's cold forehead. 'You were a brave warrior, my friend. I might have forgiven you.' He faces Cicero, who drops his eyes. 'You think me weak?'

'No, Your Highness. Your grief is natural.'

'One I seem to be letting overwhelm me. That's what bothered the captain. And in some ways, he was right. I've let this situation go on too long.'

'I don't know his reasons,' says Cicero, 'but I do know he was a good and loyal servant to the empire.'

'A bold statement.'

'Said with respect and honesty, Your Highness.'

Octavius looks again at the captain. 'Send him on his way. Let stardust take him to his next destination.'

'Full honours, Your Majesty?'

'Of course, but I can't be present. I must get ready to speak with Livia.'

LXXX

Livia runs her fingers along the pinstripe suits hanging in her wardrobe; next to them, pair after pair of red pixie boots stacked on shelves. A stock level for each of forty-two, made by tailors and cobblers on Earth – replenished monthly to keep them in pristine condition. She should be thinking about Octavius, but the only thing filling her head is Athos and the way he stroked her palm. That playful gleam in his eyes; the open flirtation of his banter. It's obvious he wants something more, but that has never been an option, not for her. Octavius has instilled duty as her priority, but what sort of existence is that, even for a god?

With her hand, she brushes the coat of one of the suits, easing a hairline crease from the fabric. Hiding behind an armour of pinstripes to shield her from normal life. That's what a therapist would say, but what does she care? She's a princess; an arbiter of fate. She can do what she wants. Or can she? The dream of a path opens in her mind – Athos holding her close in a cave behind a cascading waterfall; breathless as they run hand in hand across a planet of ice castles; laughing into the wind as they carpet-chase pods of dolphins across mint-green oceans. And then there's children. Lots of them, but, most importantly, an heir to the throne. How can Octavius object to a grandson who will carry on his realm? She suspects a tinge of disappointment hit her father when Helena delivered a daughter. Although, to be fair, it has never shown. She smiles and turns towards the orb, which levitates behind her. 'Is any of it possible?'

'He likes you.'

'But could it work?'

The orb blinks but stays silent.

Livia turns again to face the suits. 'Perhaps when the game concludes. How ill is Octavius?'

'He grieves Helena and worries about you.'

'I wish we could stop falling out, but every time I think about him and what he did, my blood boils.'

'It's not easy for him, either. He knows how foolish he was, but someone betrayed him and—'

'What if no one betrayed him and his own stupidity let him down and killed my mother?'

'Only he can find the answer to that question.'

She runs her hand across the suits again. 'Which means talking to him, before he brings the empire crashing down.'

*

From her throne, Livia stares through the glass atrium ceiling and tries to count the ubiquitous flashes in the starry sky. She's heard gods say they're bored with the view. They'll gather to watch a comet blasting through the cosmos or a meteor shower storming through space, but the everyday existence of a galaxy is treated as white noise by some – taken for granted. Perhaps, thinks Livia, it's her human genes that fill her with wonder. She concentrates again on the view of Octavius's empire, thinks how he gave her a chance to make a mark, to stake her claim for inheritance, but now it's all under threat.

In front of her, an eerie silence has settled as the ecclesia watch Phillippa stride up and down, speedily coaxing yarn through weft and warp threads onto a gold-framed loom. At her side, heads twitching, the goshawks wait patiently on an oak perch; next to them, the teller sisters, Paloma and Sini, work in unison to spin raw flax, sweating under pressure to keep up with Phillippa's pace as she draws her images to predict the fates.

Sebastian enters the atrium, bows once, walks over to Livia and hands her a note, which she reads.

'You're sure about this?'

'Absolutely,' says Sebastian.

Phillippa stops weaving and faces her audience. 'It is decided.'

Livia and Athos stand and walk over to the loom, closely followed by the rest of the ecclesia. Everyone peers at the woven scene. Two Goliaths, bushy beards, cross-legged, clad in fur pelts, facing each other above the clouds, on the summit of a mountain. In front of them a chessboard, ebony and ivory pieces laid out in a start-game position.

'Wrath and Octavius?' says Livia.

'Obviously,' says Phillippa, brushing down her lion skin and picking up each of her goshawks in turn, returning them to her shoulders. 'Are you saying it's not clear?'

'They're playing chess?'

'Another game to decide the fate of the empress,' says Athos. 'That we can all live with.'

Phillippa steps forward and fans across the loom with her right hand. 'You're missing the whole picture.'

They all stare again.

'But that's—'

'You, Athos. Battle sword drawn and striking, shield engaged, full combat pose, but it's not clear who you're fighting. And there you are, Princess, being chased across the sky by a posse of Wrath's thunder clouds; and you, Timus—'

'Where?' says Timus, pushing himself forwards to get a closer view.

'Typical. On the edge of the ocean, directing from a distance.'

'It's called a plan, Athos. Not that a brute like you would understand.'

'You're saying war?' says Livia. 'Then why the chess game?'

'Those are the options,' says Phillippa, smiling at Athos and Timus, who face up to each other at the side of the loom. 'The fates are unclear which resolution Wrath and Octavius will choose. No one will want to back the wrong team. Which is why you need to convince your father.'

'He'll decide for himself.'

'Maybe it's time you tested that. These options are games, but one will result in slaughter, possibly the end of the empire.'

Livia sits back on her throne. 'Talking to Octavius won't be easy.'

Phillippa takes a step towards her. 'Then the empire will fall.'

'You don't understand.'

'I understand your anger at Helena's fate, but this is an opportunity to put things right. You have a responsibility.'

'Even if Octavius agrees,' says Athos, 'there's no guarantee Wrath will choose the chess option.'

'He likes his games,' says Bernard.

Everyone turns towards the monk.

'You dare speak of a god?' says Timus.

'I'm an ecclesia member, Timus. Here by right.'

'In name only, and that'll be short-lived when Octavius discovers—'

'Discovers what? I'm not the only one who has some explaining to do when the emperor returns. Shouldn't we all be pulling together in this moment of crisis?'

'He's right,' says Athos. 'This isn't the time for arguing amongst ourselves. You must speak to your father, Princess.'

Livia looks down at the piece of paper in her lap. 'Not with the way the game progresses.'

'The game?' says Timus. 'Irrelevant now, surely. What's happened?'

'Octavius intends to intervene directly.'

'He can't. That's—'

'Against the rules, but he's decided.'

'And you'll oppose him?'

'I've no choice. I can't abandon my champion.'

LXXXI

Mary sits on the grass bank and watches as Rico walks up and down the glade, prodding away at the soggy ground with a tree branch he's found in the undergrowth.

'There's nothing here,' he shouts.

'We need to wait. It was never going to be obvious.'

'We're on the clock, remember. They could be here any second.'

She reaches into her pocket, pulls out the silver fob watch and flicks open the lid.

04:22; 04:21…

'Time is now irrelevant.'

'Jethro,' she says, turning towards the voice. 'I knew you'd appear.'

The smoke human hovers at the edge of the wood, the outline of his Afro hair barely visible through bleary fog. 'I don't have long.'

She stands up and walks over to him. 'You look sad. Has something happened?'

'The princess will explain. She's on her way.'

'Jethro,' shouts Rico, racing over. 'We've been waiting for you. There's no sign of—'

'Something's happened,' says Mary. 'The princess is coming.'

'She's coming here?'

'The emperor as well,' says Jethro. 'And the Jinga are already watching.'

They scan the glade, trying to spot their pursuers. 'But the crystals,' says Rico. 'We have them. We need to find the well.'

Jethro drifts back into the trees. 'The well will appear when you lay out the crystals, but the emperor and princess will decide its potency. Everything has changed.'

And with that he puffs out of sight.

'Not good news,' says Rico. 'Should we just sit and wait?'

Mary stares at the edge of the woods. 'He looked different.'

'I'm guessing a falling-out, which puts us right in the middle.'

'The well will appear if we lay out the crystals. That's what he said. Let's at least do that.'

'What's the point? The princess and emperor will decide if it works.'

'I'd rather keep busy. Come on.'

She strides towards the backpacks, which they've dumped in the centre of the glade.

Rico trudges after her.

*

Dappled sunlight spots each labradorite shape, making the amber translucent and the veins pulsate as Mary lays them out on the grass.

She sets them in a line – square, triangle, football. Nothing.

'Do you think there's an order?' she says.

Rico shrugs from his sitting place on the bank, scanning the horizon. 'They're coming. I can feel them.'

'I thought I was the one with premonitions.'

'This isn't a game, Mary. We're in trouble.'

'I thought it was a game. Isn't that the point?'

'You've never been on the receiving end—'

'I just don't see how moping is going to help. At least this way, we're ready.'

She rolls the triangle out of the middle, swapping it with the football.

Still nothing.

'Oh, sod it,' she says, kicking the square. 'I give up.'

Rico walks over and hugs her. 'You've tried every order,' he says, looking at the crystals. 'I don't know what else you can do. Perhaps the flow isn't right. A bit like the ring.'

'You think it might have something to do with us?'

'I don't know. Maybe.'

'But things are better between us, aren't—'

He pulls her into his arms and kisses her.

She reaches up and touches his cheek. 'I thought I told you never to interrupt me,' she says, pulling his head down and kissing him, this time squeezing him tight against her body. She pushes him away. 'Wait. What did you say?'

'About us?'

'About the flow not being right. That's it. A straight line breaks the connection. They need to be laid out...' She lets go of him, bends down, shifts the crystals – the triangle against the square; the square touching the triangle; and, finally, the circle against both – an unbroken link.

She steps back.

A rumble bubbles through the ground; a crack scars the grass, and, *whoosh*, the earth falls away. Another rumble. A round wall, a canopy, a bucket on a rope, all rise to the surface and slot together in front of their eyes. Finally, silence, and there it is, like it's been there since the beginning of time.

They race over and peer into its depths.

'You did it,' says Rico.

A new noise from the forest makes them both turn.

The shadows in front of them thud out a battle beat on shields.

LXXXII

Octavius stands behind a line of Jinga, his arms folded, watching the two humans. Behind him a posse of glass pods, like a row of stalagmites, their transport to the planet's surface. At his side, Penelope strides up and down, glad to be out of her cage. She stretches her slender human legs, twitches her bird crown feathers and blinks her eyes. 'The gangster is close?' asks Octavius, stroking the harpy's head when she nudges his arm.

'He hides in the trees,' says Cicero, pointing to the top of the hill.

'He mustn't escape.'

'You're sure the princess will come?'

'Word will have reached her. She can't ignore my direct intervention.'

He steps forward, lightly touching the backs of two Jinga, who stand to one side and let their emperor pass into the glade. A warrior's urge fills his head as he crouches and pulls at a blade of grass. Instinctively, he wants to ride into the game on his winged serpent, razor flames belching, assert his authority, but he needs to tread carefully and not lose face.

'You look troubled, Your Highness,' says Cicero, resting a hand gently on his shoulder. 'Is there anything I can do to help?'

'Your loyalty is touching, my friend. I'm about to take a gamble, and I'm uncertain of the result.'

'With the empress?'

'Everything from now is about the empress.'

A boom over their heads makes them look upwards.

Octavius turns to the Jinga. 'Be ready.'

Cicero prods his spectacles up his nose, shields his eyes and peers into the sky, tracking a slim crack of white light arcing across the sun. Another boom and a swarm of black pushes through and heads towards them from the horizon. 'What are they?'

'Soul-rugs, Cicero. Livia makes a grand entrance. She does as I expected and brings the ecclesia with her.'

'A brave move.'

'It's in her genes,' says Octavius, smiling.

LXXXIII

Fats knows an endgame when he sees one.

In front of him, the champion and his girl stand frozen next to a well, staring at a line of warriors. Across from them, a bloke in a wrap-around animal skin who couldn't look more like a god if he had it tattooed on his forehead. Bushy white beard and hair, Goliath body – an all-powerful, supreme being. The image of deity fed to Fats all his life since Sunday school. He remembers the princess, with her pinstripe suit and red pixie boots. A stylish break with tradition. She must take after her mother. The silver halo is a giveaway, though. If that wasn't enough, a buzz of fucking Axminster with figures kneeling, spiralling towards the ground, looking for a landing spot. It all adds up to a stand-off.

He concentrates again on Rico and Mary. Why aren't they jumping into the well? The crystals are sat in a hippy-shit circle, but they're just standing there, fixed like lambs to the slaughter. Something must have shifted again.

He strokes the ring and wonders if it still works. Not for him. He knows that. But the well, the crystals...

'Fun time over,' says a voice behind him.

'You took your time,' says Fats, turning. 'What happened to the hat?'

Hector steps forwards, two more warriors at his back. 'If you run, I'll kill you.'

Fats feels breath on his face as the Jinga reaches him. He looks again at the glade. 'That the boss man down there?'

'It's the emperor, and, for now, he wants you in one piece.'

'What about his daughter? I'm assuming she lost—'

'You talk too much,' spits Hector, grabbing Fats' throat.

'I see I've pissed you off,' croaks Fats.

LXXXIV

Livia adjusts her kneeling balance to look at the figures on the ground.

'The emperor has company,' says Sebastian, seated in front of her, subtly shifting his weight from one leg to the other, steering them to their landing.

She nods but is distracted by the soul-rug, which she strokes, conscious of lost humans woven into its intricate threads, waiting to be released to limbo. Swirls of pattern ripple with life; colours bleed into each other. She's learnt to switch off the begging screams of the dead, pleading for another chance. She looks behind her and sees the ecclesia cross-legged on their rugs, following her route. Darius rests his winged feet to hitch a ride with Bernard; Phillippa flies alone, her goshawks screeching with excitement as wind gushes through their feathers; Athos and Timus close behind.

'The rugs ensure we arrive in style,' says Sebastian.

'We should have come alone,' says Livia.

'The ecclesia was never staying away, Your Highness, and the emperor has his Jinga.'

'Theatre. We've lived with it for far too long.'

A movement at the edge of the glade draws her attention.

Three Jinga warriors walk into view, pushing a human male ahead of them.

'The gangster,' says Sebastian. 'Now everyone is here.'

'Yes,' says Livia, looking towards Rico and Mary, who are still standing next to the well. 'Their fates will be decided by Octavius. The game has achieved nothing.'

Sebastian faces her. 'It's brought this conversation to a head. I doubt it would have happened otherwise.'

'Take us down,' says Livia.

LXXXV

Mary watches Rico.

Terror etches across his face as he takes in the Jinga and, what she knows from her dreams to be their pursuer, the emperor – the one who wants to capture them for the sake of a game. Four rugs spiral downwards, hover for a second over the grass and then slide-land in the glade. 'Are you okay?' whispers Mary, squeezing Rico's hand.

He opens his mouth, but no words come out.

'We'll get through this,' she says but hears nervousness in her voice, a slight tremor trickle. She worries about what trauma ignites in his head, whether it's the same as his panic attack on the beach. She squeezes his hand again.

'There's nothing we can do,' he says.

'We can hope,' she says, kissing him on the cheek.

He nods towards the first rug. 'The princess.'

She looks at the woman being helped to her feet by an eight-foot-tall albino. A pinstripe suit and red pixie boots doesn't scream supreme leader of the afterlife. 'Not what I expected. I'm assuming the rest of them are gods.'

'The ecclesia.'

'With us or against us?'

'No idea, but they came with the princess.'

She watches as they disembark: a monk in a swirling cassock, who looks tired and beaten; a muscle man adjusting his height from human to tree canopy size, in some kind of body stretching regime after his journey; a woman wearing a lion skin, a goshawk on each shoulder; a winged cherub fluttering above them; a pot-bellied buddha growling at everyone. Mary laughs.

Rico gives her a puzzled look.

'The things we now take as normal,' she says, 'but it's all bonkers.'

'Here's Fats,' he says, putting his arm round her shoulder and pointing towards a gap in the trees.

Fats stumbles into view, three Jinga at his back.

'Now what?' says Mary.

'It doesn't look friendly,' says Rico.

LXXXVI

Octavius hesitates, unsure of his next steps.

He has an overwhelming desire to take Livia in his arms, kiss the top of her head, make shushing noises to calm her, but none of that has been normal since the snatching of Helena. She blames him; he blames himself, and it's all compounded by a quest for power. He wants to hug her and whisper fairy stories but pushes the thought away, fearing rejection. For now, they are embittered, but all that must change.

'Livia,' he calls, stepping forwards into the glade. 'You look well.'

He stops walking when he sees no response. She stays rooted to the spot, the manservant albino alongside, the ecclesia at her back. He turns to Cicero. 'No reaction. What do I do?'

'She awaits you, Your Highness.'

'Tradition says we meet halfway. She could at least say something. Should I have my Jinga with me? This is ridiculous.' He faces Livia again. 'I've come in good faith,' he calls. 'To resolve this game and talk about your mother. Do you not want the same thing?'

She looks at the ground and then back at him, turns and says something to Sebastian and he nods. 'I'll meet you, Father,' she calls, 'but only you.'

'Wait here,' says Octavius to Cicero, walking forwards again.

Livia walks towards him, leaving Sebastian and the ecclesia watching closely.

LXXXVII

Fats gently tugs against the ropes securing his hands behind his back and feels the yarn burn into his skin. For some reason, he's thinking about Ricky No Toes and wondering where he is in this fucked-up world. He regrets grassing him up to Jean, a coward's trick. He should have waited, found a different way to even the score, something more in keeping with the gangster's code of ethics. He'll tell him that if their paths ever cross.

He gulps twice. There's a gritty soreness in his throat since the Jinga let go of him and he could do with a glug of water, but he's gauging the right time to ask. He calculates pissing the Jinga off again could probably wait. The bloke's looking for an excuse to kick the shit out of someone, anyone. Fats knows he's annoying, that's part of his charm, helps him survive, but the force of the Jinga's squeeze, the unnecessary tightness of the rope, tells him there's more going on. He's done it himself, put in a couple of extra kicks because he's pissed about something else, usually a woman. He guesses the Jinga's not happy with his job. A weakness, something to exploit if he ever gets a chance to speak.

The scene unfolding in front of him is exactly what he thought would happen. What the pirates call a parley: take off your spurs; lay your cards on the table; leave your guns at the door; make sure everyone leaves the party with a balloon.

Him, the champion, the woman, all forgotten, for now.

He touches the ring with his little finger.

'Patience,' he tells himself.

'Keep your eyes forward,' snarls Hector.

'Whatever you say,' croaks Fats.

LXXXVIII

Livia studies Octavius, noting new wrinkles drawn deep across his forehead, a knotty beard, lank hair, tired eyes. She has an urge to reach out and touch his cheek, thinks how furious her mother would be at his unkempt appearance. 'You want to talk?'

He holds his ground, arms across his chest about four feet in front of her. 'This game needs to end.'

'I agree. Let my champion and his girl go. They deserve another chance.'

'You want me to appear weak.'

'They made it through the hunting ground, found the well. Your direct intervention is not allowed.'

'My mercy has allowed them to reach this point. I could have captured them hours ago. And this gangster you've brought in. Is that permitted?'

She looks round the glade and then back at Octavius. Her mind drifts, brings up her mother's image. She feels the pang of loss that always engulfs her when she remembers what he did. 'You can do what you want. You usually do.' She starts to walk back towards Sebastian.

'Wait,' says Octavius.

She stops, keeping her back to him. 'I'm assuming my reign is over.'

No reply, but she hears footsteps, his breathing coming closer, and then feels his hand on her shoulder. 'I've seen your mother,' he says.

'That's impossible. She's beyond your reach.'

'In a dream. She asked me to get her back.'

'You intend to war with Wrath. Have you gone mad? That ruins everything.'

'Not if we join forces. We need to reconcile our differences.'

She faces him. 'I'll never forgive you.'

He reaches out and takes her hand. 'I've punished myself for my recklessness. It shouldn't have happened. The smoke brothers—'

'Another lie. They're family and had nothing to do with your negligence.'

'If not them, the monk, but I had everything—'

'You're to blame. Yet, even now, you deny responsibility.' She frees her hand and walks away. 'You risked my mother's life over a game of cards, treated her like rubbish.'

He flashes a look at the ecclesia and then at the Jinga. They must have heard. He can't ignore it. He stretches to tree height and steps forward two paces, coming to her side. 'You will listen to me.'

'Why? Because you're a god? Go ahead, strike me down. I can't match you with my half-human body, but at least I'm not a coward.'

A gasp echoes across the glade.

Octavius raises his fist.

Livia closes her eyes.

LXXXIX

The ecclesia wait in a line, looking as though they're holding their breath. Sebastian steps forward, but Athos puts an arm out to stop him.

'I need to help—'

'You can do nothing. The emperor will choose his next action.'

'What she said is unforgiveable,' says Phillippa.

'And yet she still lives.'

Sebastian registers Athos's words. 'What's the emperor doing?'

'Deciding. This is between a father and daughter.'

Darius flutters above them. 'The moment has passed. We can all breathe again.'

XC

Livia feels him standing in front of her.

'Open your eyes,' says Octavius.

She does as he asks.

He's back to human size.

'You've spared me.'

'You're my daughter.'

'I need to understand. You owe me that much.'

'I've tried over and over to work it out. In my mind, there was no risk. Everything had been thought of—'

'And yet it went wrong. There's only one way for us to know.'

'I can't—'

'Then it will never be resolved. Only you can authorise a recall.'

XCI

Fats welcomes the distraction of two blackbirds playing tug of war with a worm, stretching its slimy body, revolving it like a skipping rope. The smaller of the birds suddenly releases its grip and the other bird zooms skywards, the worm dangling between its legs.

What a freak show, he thinks as he looks towards the line of chaise longues at the edge of the woods, where the ecclesia have taken their repose alongside Cicero. Next to them, Livia and Octavius sit on platinum thrones, while the Jinga circle the glade, apart from the three pushing Fats around, who stand guard next to the humans.

He grins at Rico and Mary, sitting next to him on the seating stage. 'Are you okay?' he mouths to Mary, who's at his side.

'Yes,' she mouths back, touching his arm.

He slides the ring off his finger, glad to be rid of the ropes, waits for a second to make sure the guards are focused on the scene in front of them and then carefully passes it across. 'Just in case,' he mouths.

Mary clutches the ring, a puzzled look on her face.

Livia stands.

Everyone turns in her direction.

'It's time to start,' she says. 'The emperor has agreed to replay the game that sealed my mother's fate, but first, we need everyone present who has an interest in that day.'

She holds her hands skywards and draws them slowly back, causing the clouds to part and a thick fog to puff through. It swirls and reforms into four smoke humans who drift to Earth and take their positions, bobbing at the side of the stage: Jethro in the centre, his plume of Afro hair hanging over him like a feather. He smiles a battered yellow-teeth smile towards the monk. Bernard turns his head away and ignores him.

'Let the show commence,' says Livia, retaking her seat.

A gong sounds from somewhere in the woods and the teller sisters emerge through the trees, both carrying brooms, and stand in front of the thrones. Livia nods at them and they sweep the ground in circles, Paloma leading the way, Sini resweeping her path. Round and round, tracking each other, upping their pace on each turn, dust bellowing until they become a blur of brush and body. And then they stop, coming to a halt at the same moment, stomp their feet and chant over and over. No words, just a high-pitched wail.

Something scuttles across the circle they've created.

Fats shifts to the edge of his seat to get a closer look. What is that? It looks like a carpet, rippling about in waves, but then he realises it's not one thing but thousands: an army of tiny red and white spiders trampling over and under each other.

Paloma and Sini step out of the circle.

Livia stands and holds up her arms again. Immediately, the spiders spread upwards, through the branches, interweaving, more and more of them emerging from the ground, higher and higher, pile upon pile until they reach the canopy of the trees. And then they spread through the undergrowth, linking tree to tree, until the teller sisters bang their brooms on the ground and Livia drops her arms.

Fats looks at Mary and Rico, who are transfixed on a square mass of wriggling red and white spiders squirming in front of them.

A second gong.

The spiders weave into each other to form an opaque block.

Images bubble to its surface.

Two gods sitting at a card table.

'Do you think they'd be pissed if I ask for popcorn?' Fats whispers to Mary.

Hector pokes him in the back with a stick.

Fats gives him a salute and turns back to the spider screen.

*

The frames unpack themselves one by one.

Fats has seen better films, but he knows this one could save his afterlife and give him another shot in the living world. He concentrates, detaches his surroundings, the game and the fact that he's dead. Just two blokes playing cards. That's how he needs to think. The boss man looking for something, jolting the clips scene by scene, controlling them with a rub of his fingers. The daughter looks pissed, so Fats guesses the hand didn't go well. *Sealed my mother's fate.* He's seen some crazy bets, but who the fuck stakes their wife?

Boss man walks over to the spider screen for a closer look.

Fats wants to do the same. A feeling in his water tells him there's a reprieve here. If only he can answer whatever question these fuckers are asking. He wants to punch his thigh, get his concentration on track, but rules that out when he feels Jinga breath on his neck. Instead, he digs his nails into his arm. 'Watch, Fats,' he tells himself. 'Watch.'

Harder. Harder.

Click. Click. Click.

Two blokes playing cards.

Four helpers; Goatee man unseals the pack; Baldy shuffles; Afro deals…

He looks at the smoke humans and then back at the screen. They're the same. Piercings restacks. Managers of the game. Why so many? Weirdos loving their drama. What happened? Whatever it was, smokies got the blame, had their bodies lifted. But now there's doubt. There must be something.

Watch. Watch.

He digs harder and stares again at the clicking images. They've gone back to the start. If only he can find out…

'Father,' says Livia, making Fats jump, 'we've been through these four times now. There's nothing. You simply lost.'

'There must be something,' says Octavius, rubbing away, keeping his eyes fixed on the screen.

She stands. 'At least we know the smoke humans were blameless. They can be restored.'

He ignores her and carries on rubbing.

Click. Click. Click…

'Stop,' shouts Fats.

Hector hits him across the back of the head. 'Silence,' he growls, going to hit him again.

'Wait,' says Livia, striding across the glade. She reaches the humans and grabs Fats' face. 'This had better not be bullshit.'

'Bottom corner, right at the start,' he splutters.

Livia turns to Octavius, who clicks furiously back through the frames.

'Show me,' she says, dragging Fats to his feet and pushing him towards the screen.

He stumbles across the grass, reeling from the clout dished out by the Jinga, praying it's there, starts to doubt. Spare spiders wriggle up the tree barks, making him walk faster to get away from them. He reaches Octavius.

'You've seen something, human?' snaps the emperor.

'I think—'

'Point,' says Livia, coming to his side.

He peers at the frozen frame. The right one, and, yes, there it is. A whoosh of adrenalin fills his body. He grins at the gods. 'You'll need to zoom in.'

Octavius rubs his fingers.

Father and daughter study the spot.

'A switch,' says Fats. 'He traded the unsealed pack right at the start.'

Everyone turns towards the chaise longues.

The one in the centre is empty.

A soul-rug disappears over the horizon.

XCII

Jethro pokes a stick into the fire and listens to the wood crackle as the flames take hold. He kicks at a charred log that has rolled out of the ashes, stamps it back into the heat with the heel of his walking boot; rubs his hands together and touches the wall, basking in the joy of solidity. Crickets sound a dawn chorus, and he walks to the mouth of the cave to suck in the early morning air and scan the view.

He starts with the lake in the pit of the valley, sparkles dazzling as the sun's rays dance off the water's surface. He thinks of the years spent chanting at its shoreline, asking the gods for forgiveness. For what? They'd done no wrong, but he refuses to be bitter. Too much time has already been wasted. Around him are undulating hillsides, some just bare rock with the occasional cactus sucking life from dried-out earth, others lush with forests of eucalyptus trees. No one knows why the difference. They all get the same weather. His eyes rest on the sky. Auburn. His favourite colour. Melancholy with a tinge of hope. Over the years he's seen every shade – fiery reds, washed-out greens, glorious blues – populated with comets, shooting stars, joyful sunsets and sunrises. He recalls his conversations with the clouds, keeping him sane while he existed in gaseous form. Brothers in arms he called them. It helped him survive.

He turns his gaze to the centre hill. Rhododendron bushes smothering the ground, parted by a gushing stream. Hidden from view, and at the end of a meandering path, a crashing waterfall, cascading from a summit lake. Shooting up from the hill's peak is the atrium's entrance: a glass tower disappearing into the heavens; air bubbles floating up and down, giving humans a mode of transport to ride and a way of gulping breath on their journey to serve the gods. Access is by invitation only, but he has no desire to visit. Not yet.

'Feels good, doesn't it?' says Michael, coming to his side and handing over a mug of steaming coffee. He rests a hand on his brother's shoulder.

Jethro smiles at him and looks back at the twins, curled up in their separate sleeping bags – Thomas facing the ceiling, blowing purr snores at the craggy rocks above; Alfie on his side, towards the fire, flames reflecting in his lip studs.

A magpie lands on the ledge above the cave, and then another.

'Good sign,' says Michael.

Jethro takes a sip of coffee. 'You make your own fate.'

'Maybe, but something changed our fortune. I can't believe it happened.'

'We survived, and the evidence could not be disputed.'

'The human saved—'

'He saved himself, which is what we must do.'

Michael nods towards the back of the cave, furthest away from the comfy heat. Another sleeping bag, a heap of a body curled tight in a monk's cassock. 'I'm astonished he escaped so lightly. He must have known all along.'

'Let's just enjoy the view,' says Jethro, staring again at the horizon and taking in a deep breath.

XCIII

Fats taps his foot on the base of the bar stool, trying to keep up with the rhythm of The Tourists' 'So Good to Be Back Home Again'. He's loaded the jukebox, and Elton John's 'I'm Still Standing' is next up.

'Another drink, buddy?' says the barman.

'Keep them coming,' says Fats.

The barman pours a slug of crème de menthe into a whisky tumbler followed by a couple of shots of Pernod. He whizzes the glass along the bar, a beaming grin on his face. Fats laughs, happy to see the cowboy style give the barman so much pleasure.

'I thought we'd lost you,' says the barman. 'That bloke looked like he wanted your skin. All sorted now?'

'We made up. Nothing I couldn't handle.'

'Thanks for the tip. That one's on the house.'

Fats holds up the glass and carries on tapping his foot.

All sorted. Bullshit. He got lucky. Taking the

breaks when they come and riding out shitstorms. That's the secret to life. He swirls the liqueur round the glass, takes a sip and lets the alcohol burn the back of his throat before swallowing. Dead, but now alive. His drop into the well landed him in a heap back on his streets. A second chance. He hadn't looked back when the princess nodded, not even to wink a goodbye at the champion's girl. He'd like to have, but that fucking albino just snarled at him to go.

He checks out the bar. Empty. The barman looks happy to see him – to see anyone. Right on cue, the door opens, bringing a cold draught from the streets. A blonde, wearing a black thigh-length dress with a zip up the front, a raspberry beret and a green woollen jacket with Dennis the Menace and Gnasher badges pinned to the lapels. She smiles at him and takes a seat at the opposite end of the bar.

What next? Jean is out the picture. He can hardly turn up and shout, 'Remember me?' Maybe he'll give Gemma a call. There's a vacancy now Ricky No Toes has met his maker. He can't say things like that anymore. Not now he knows the truth. The bollocks they peddle about angels and paradise. They're just as fucked up as everyone else. A new start. That's what he needs. He knows he'll have to face them again one day, but for now…

'A white wine,' says the girl with the raspberry beret.

'I'll get that,' says Fats, picking up his drink and walking to the stool next to her. He looks round the empty bar. 'This seat taken?'

She laughs.

Elton bangs out his opening chords.

XCIV

Octavius takes Cicero's hand, steps out of the rowing boat and onto the jetty. He faces the boatman, whose dark eyes look up at him from underneath the pulled-up hood of his cloak. 'A smooth journey,' says Octavius, holding out a handful of gold. 'This is for you.'

'No charge, Your Highness,' says the boatman. 'It's been a pleasure.'

'Thank you,' says Octavius, turning and climbing the steps to stand beside Cicero on the wooden boards.

They look at the sandy beach.

'The labyrinth entrance is nearby?' asks Cicero.

'It is, but the limbo keeper will help us.'

In front of them, a shore crammed with human souls, all looking in awe at the jetty, holding out their hands and wailing. 'Save me. Save me.'

'She earns her existence living here,' says Cicero.

Octavius strides along the boards. 'You get used to it. That's her job.'

Cicero follows him, wondering how they'll find a path through the mass of bodies seeking salvation. The answer comes quickly when Octavius clicks his fingers and, like a plague of cockroaches coming into contact with light, the blanket of souls scuttles from view.

At the end of the jetty, a woman, barefoot, wearing a full-length red linen dress, calls to them. 'Your Majesty. It's an honour—'

'Guide us to the entrance,' says Octavius.

'At once,' says the woman, turning and walking up the beach.

'Will Wrath keep his word and meet you alone?' says Cicero. 'I'd feel easier if we had Jinga shielding us.'

'His rules. And his chess set.'

'But you play well, Your Majesty.'

'Whatever it takes, I need to get her back.'

'And what about Athos?'

'We'll deal with him when the time comes.'

They follow the woman in silence, each of them lost in their own thoughts.

XCV

Livia leans over the plasma pool, conscious of Paloma and Sini pretending to weave their fates but making anxious glances towards her. She wishes they'd be more discreet, but she's also trying to work out if their concern is genuine. Surely, they must have known about the smoke humans, and Athos, but they said nothing. *Why didn't these things appear in their prophecies?* A deception or some elaborate manipulation by Octavius. She needs to find out, but, for now, there are more important things to address, like the ecclesia. Her skin prickles at the thought of them. Was there more they could have done? Should they have seen what was going on?

The arrogance of the ecclesia's repose has diluted to a slouch of guilt, which is the way it should be since Athos's exposure. She'd like more regret; maybe questions about themselves. But all they offer is a brooding silence, simmering in front of her. She wonders how culpable they are; if any of them aided and abetted the deception. Her standout choice would be Timus, who spends most of his time with his eyes shut and dozing, but she doubts it. He makes no secret of his love for Octavius, and his disgust of Livia's reign, but, on the other hand, she can't rule him out. He has strong views about gods marrying humans, which means he might have placed Helena in jeopardy. And then there's Phillippa, forever tugging and beseeching her goshawks. She seems less likely, caring only that the empire survives and war is avoided at all costs. The one who seems least affected is Darius, who continues to twinkle his choirboy eyes and flutter his gossip. It crosses Livia's mind they might suspect her. Her attraction to Athos was obvious, and blackening her father's name opened an opportunity, but she was a child, and they must know she would never do anything to harm her mother.

Athos. His image appears in her mind. The way he looked at her, gave her hope of something, a future. *Did it ever mean anything to him?* She curses herself for being so naïve. 'Is there news?' she snaps.

'Nothing yet,' says Sebastian, stepping forwards. 'He's said to have joined Wrath.'

'Then Octavius will track him down, bring him for trial.'

'I don't think—'

She flashes a glare at the manservant. 'Athos betrayed my mother. I want retribution.'

'He's a core member of the ecclesia, Your Highness, with many friends—'

'And I rule without restriction while Octavius pursues his quest. The ecclesia is weak. One of them betrayed the empire.'

She walks over to the window. Silver cosmic ghosts streak by as a new galaxy comes into view, untouched by gods from its day of creation, fresh planets and stars waiting to be discovered. 'This will be a good start to my realm. What news of the emperor?'

'He's reached the labyrinth,' says Sebastian.

'Let's hope he wins. My mother's fate is at stake.'

Sebastian looks at the teller sisters, who avoid eye contact and face their loom. 'The humans have settled,' he says, sounding as though he's trying in vain to find a safe subject.

'I saw, and the girl wears the ring.'

XCVI

Mary lets the screen door of their farmhouse slam shut behind her, leans on the porch rail and looks up the dirt track leading into the hills. She's waiting for Rico to return from his morning run but also hoping and praying. Everything else is here – dogs fed, watered, waggy tails; Gertie hooting from the barn's rafters – but an emptiness sucks at her, consuming her emotions.

At least we're alive, she tells herself, but it isn't enough.

She still doesn't know what happened with the princess and the emperor. All she saw was Fats jumping into the well and the albino looking in her direction and kissing his hand. It had taken a few seconds of puzzlement to realise what he meant, and she'd pulled Rico's head down, both of their lips touching the white gold at the same time.

Boom.

And here they'd landed, as though nothing had happened.

Except it had, and she hadn't had time over the last week to work it all out. She'd wanted to talk to the princess, but she'd barely looked in their direction, and Fats... Who was he? What had happened to him? Rico had shrugged his shoulders when she'd asked, but that was his way. She knew that. And what about Rico, his previous life? He's still not told her, says the timing isn't right. She wonders if he ever will.

Footsteps sound up the path.

Rico. Pounding, sweating, speeding up as he sees the end in sight. She knows he'll be disappointed to see her outside. He wants her in bed, waiting for his sweaty embrace; his jigsaw pieces back to how they should be. But she can't, not while... The princess will look after her. That's what the woman on the beach said. But surely that meant, now they were home, the best way would be to...

She can see Rico's face.

He's smiling.

A chipped-tooth smile that she hasn't seen since they came home, and it makes her skin prickle with irritation. He looks happy, but how can he be?

She wants to yell at him, remind him of what they've lost.

And now he's looking behind, pointing up the track.

A familiar grunt reaches her ears.

Wanita bounds over the brow of the hill.

Epilogue

Wrath surveys his empire through the window of his underworld atrium.

Dark planets envelop the galaxies in front of him, rolling their orbits like lumps of coal, tracked by ice-moon sisters. Long extinct but useful holding pens for sinners brought across the wailing river, Cocytus, by the ferryman, Charon. These are the lucky ones, the ones serving a minor penance, helping mine for precious metals and minerals to boost Wrath's wealth. At least they've kept a possibility of reprieve back to limbo, unlike the souls in Tartarus, his jewel in the crown dungeon of torment, from which there is no escape.

He scratches the horn in the middle of his forehead and pulls his bear skin coat tighter before taking a deep breath and sucking in energy from the bursts of explosion – frenzied volcanos vomiting plasma to the edge of atmospheres, pinpricking the dark like psychotic fireflies. The vista changes frequently. Sometimes lightning storms scar the skies; on other days, dust vortices dance across surfaces, shrouding celestial orbs in an iridescent blue, pink and yellow fog. Even the frozen moons cough methane clouds round their surface at the speed of sound. He smiles at the thought. Moons that smell of farts. This is his domain. Noxious, unstable, on the edge of extinction. Everything as it should be.

A door opens at the far end of the atrium and a human female with long blonde hair, wearing a black-and-white maid's outfit, heads towards him pushing a tea trolley.

'Ah, Dora. On time as always. What's the cake today?'

'You've a choice,' says Dora, bringing the tea trolley to a standstill in front of him. 'Ginger or carrot. Maximus is in a baking mood.'

'Any day he's not throwing pots is a good day,' says Wrath, laughing. 'Leave the trolley and we'll serve ourselves.'

'Are you sure you wouldn't like me to pour the tea?'

He waves her away with a friendly smile, and she curtsies before walking back towards the door. She stops and faces him. 'I nearly forgot. Athos wants to see you. There's news from the surface. Shall I send him through?'

'He can wait. Give him some refreshment. And ask Empress Helena to hurry before the tea gets cold.'

Dora nods and leaves the atrium.

Wrath faces the window.

News from the surface.

'It starts again,' he says to his reflection.

About the Author

Stephen Brotherton grew up in the West Midlands and now lives in Shropshire. A social worker for nearly thirty years, he currently works for the NHS, and is a member of the Bridgnorth Writers' Group.